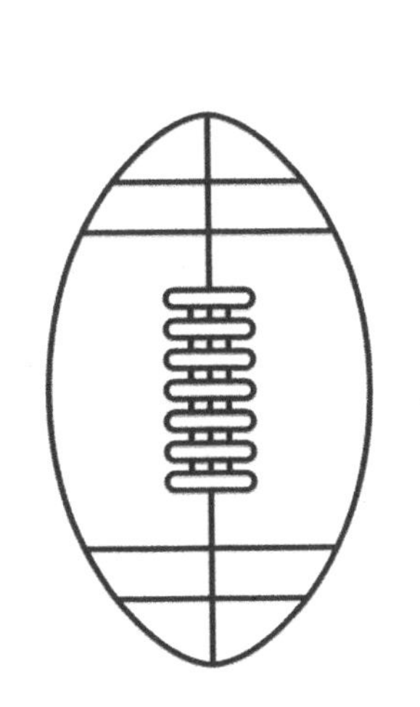

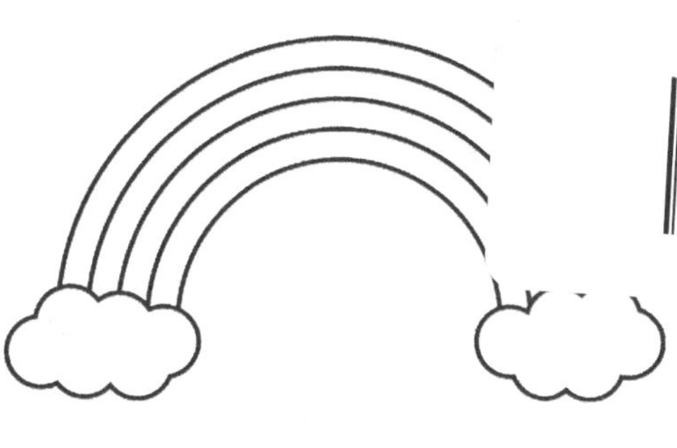

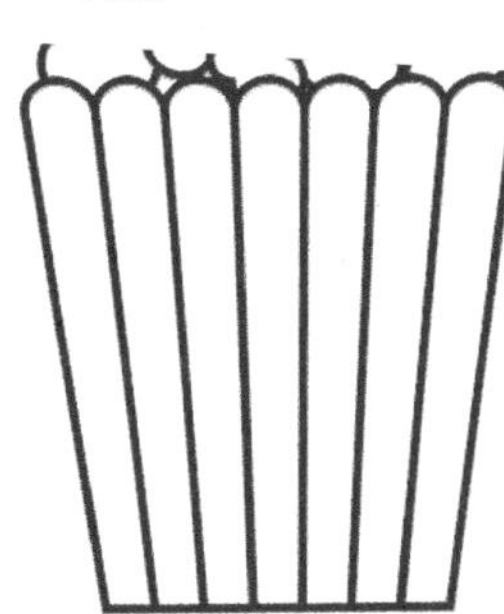

# THIS BOOK BELONGS TO

______________________________

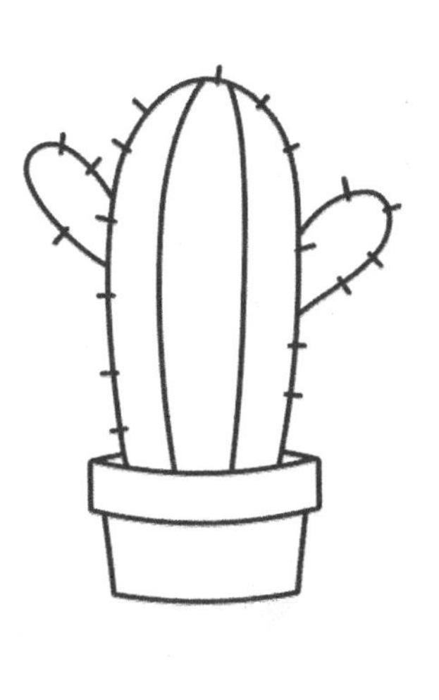

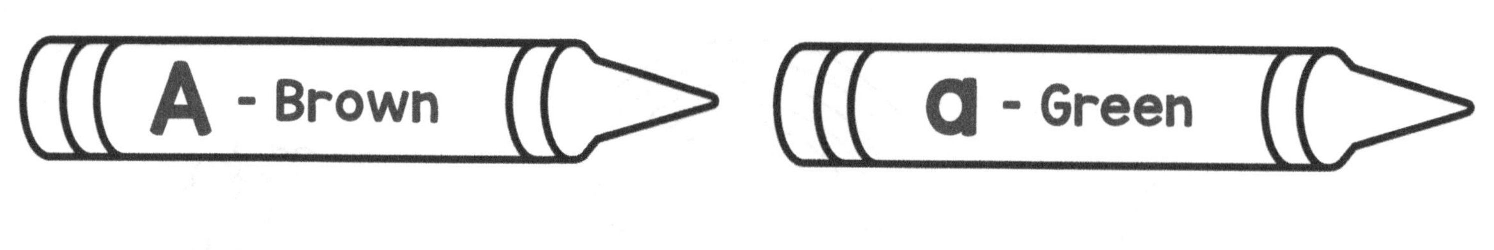
A - Brown
a - Green

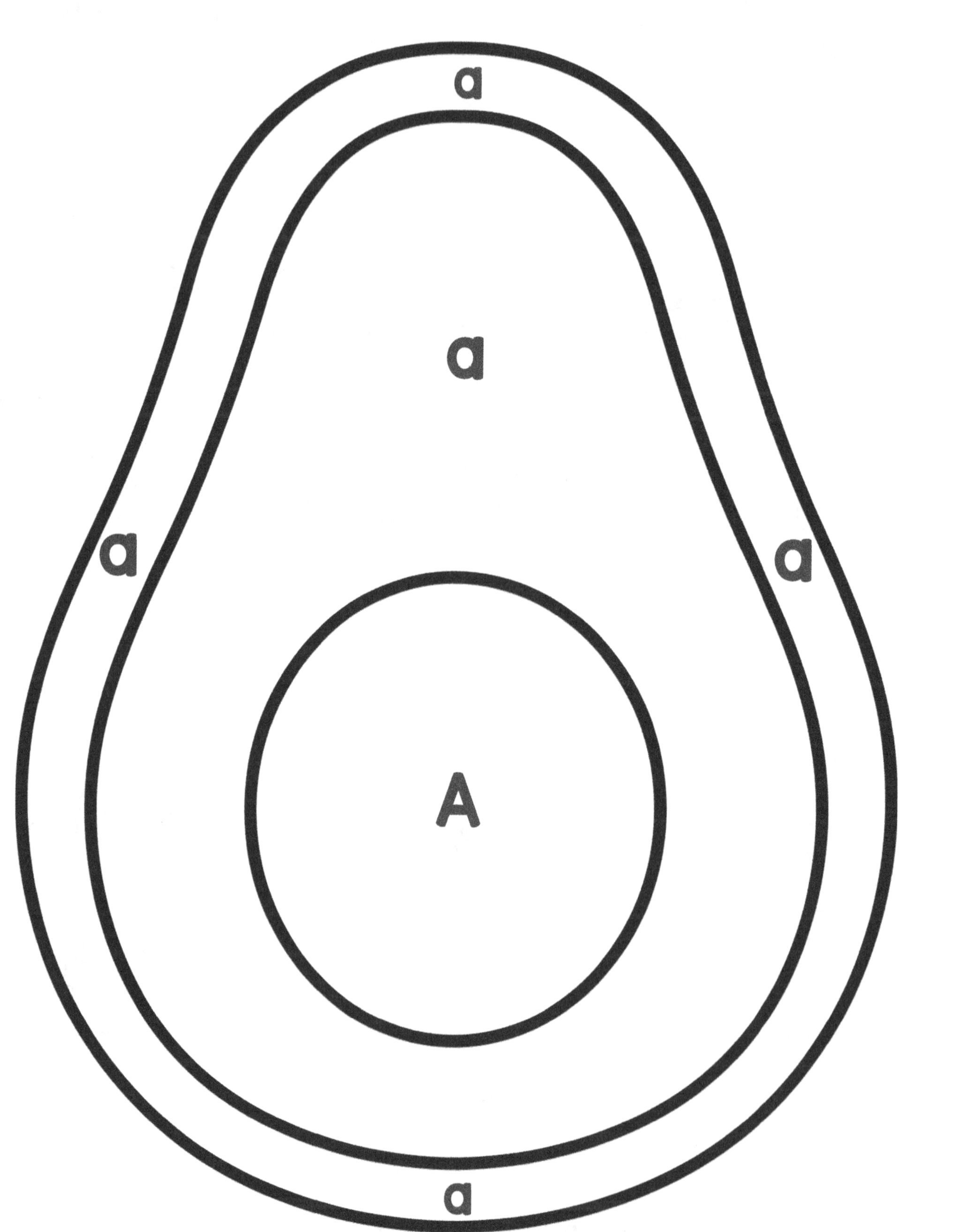
a
a
a
a
A
a

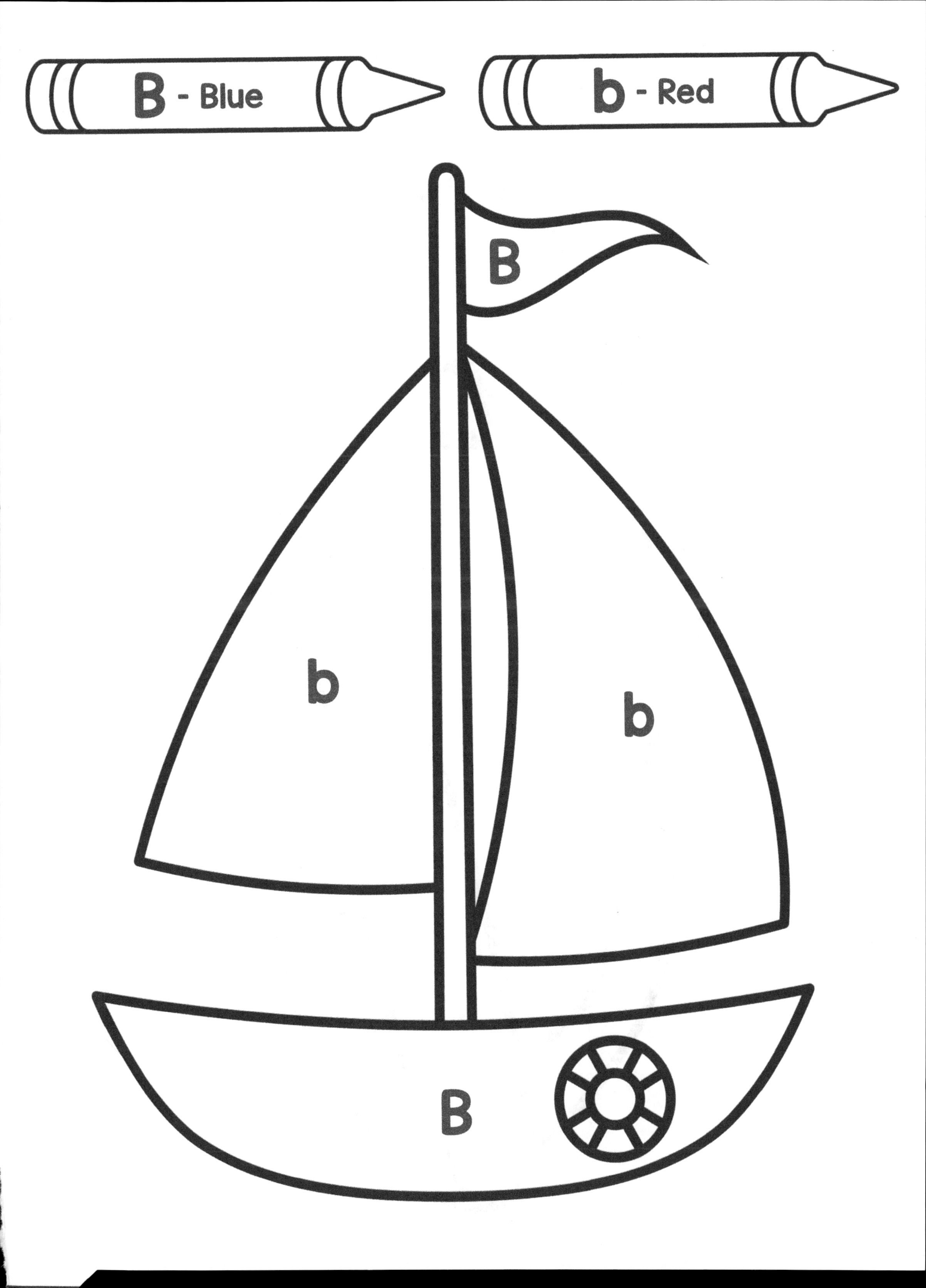
B - Blue
b - Red
B
b
b
B

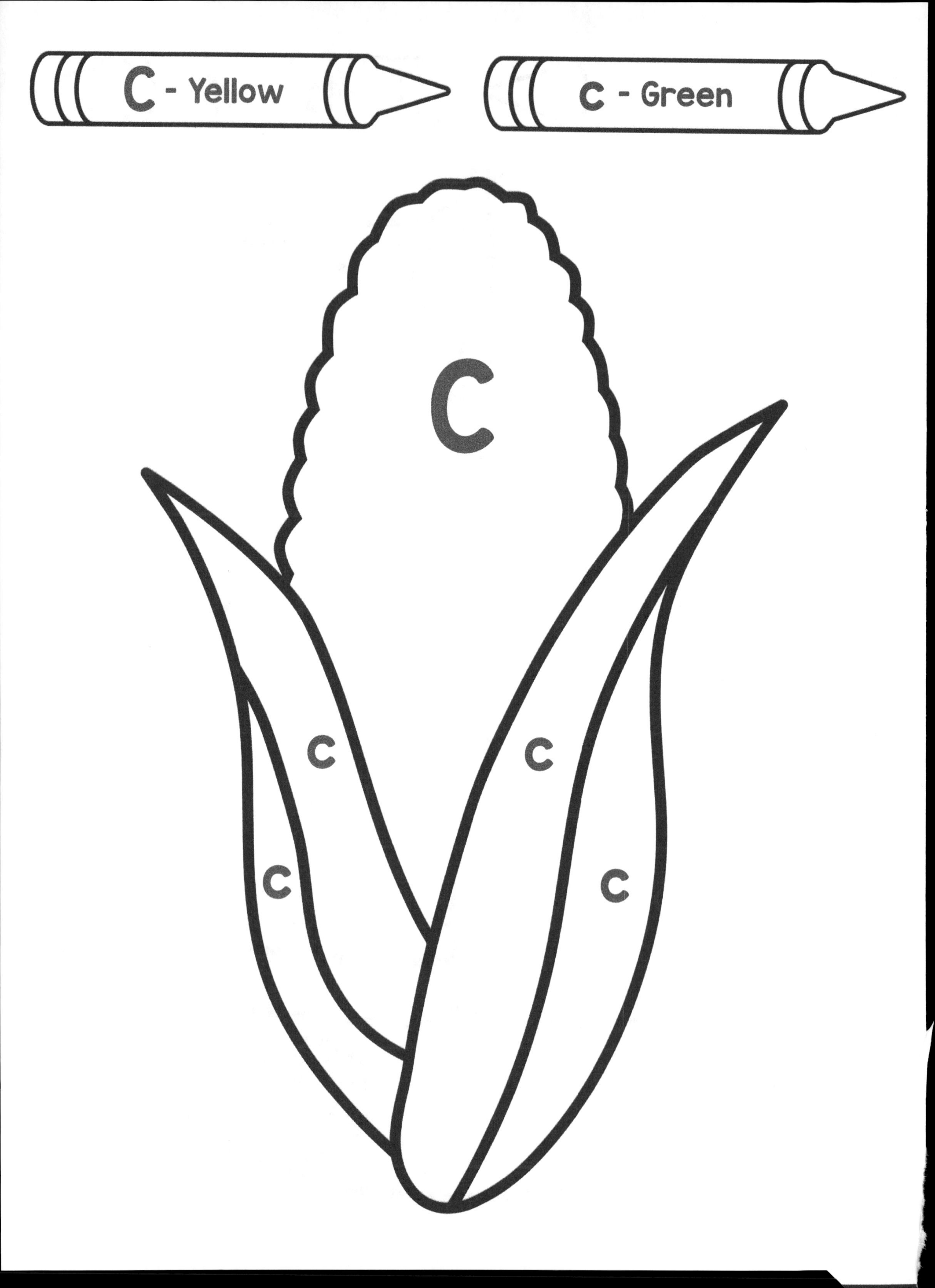
C - Yellow
c - Green
C
c
c
c
c

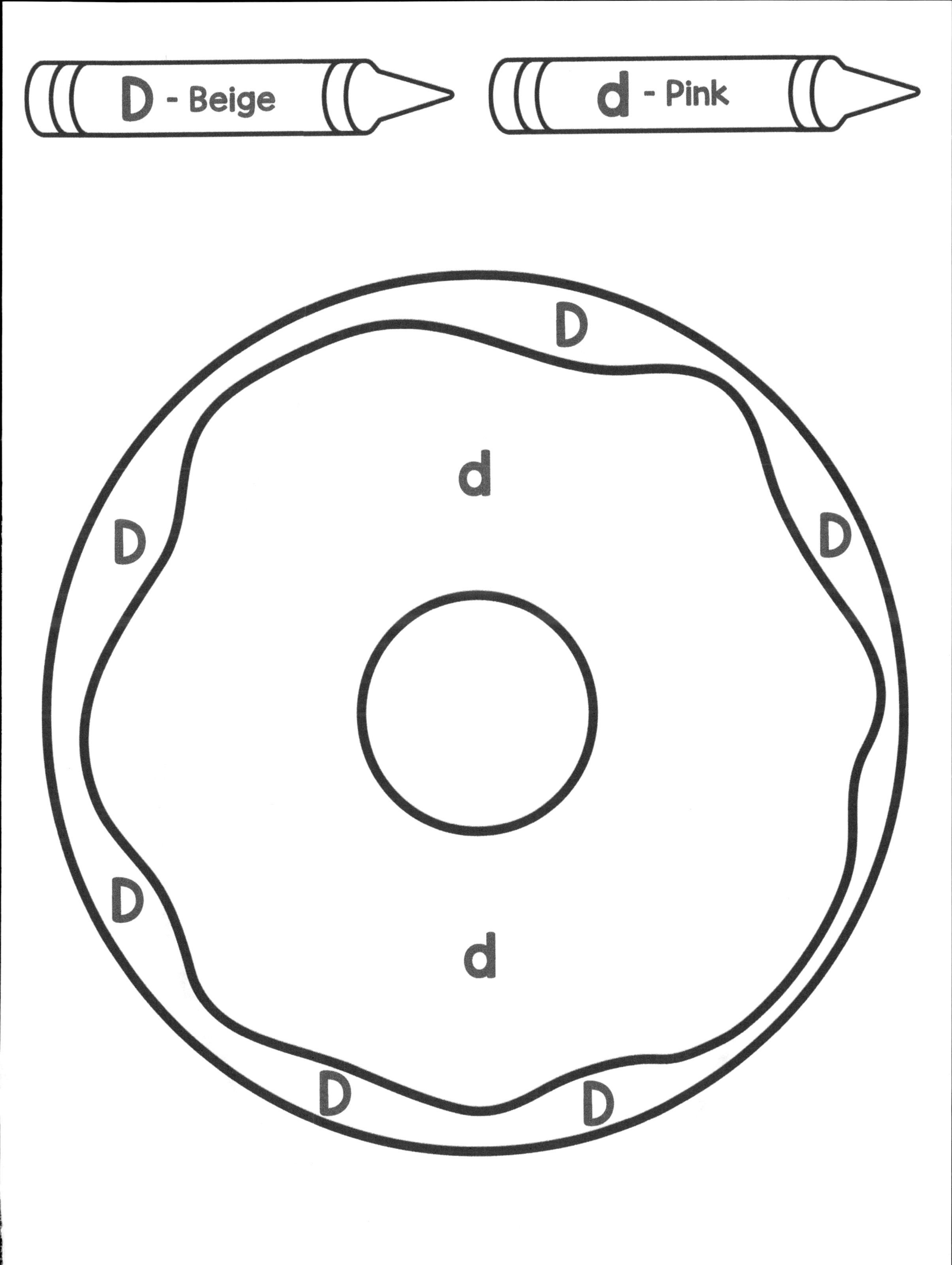
D - Beige
d - Pink
D
d
D
D
D
d
D
D

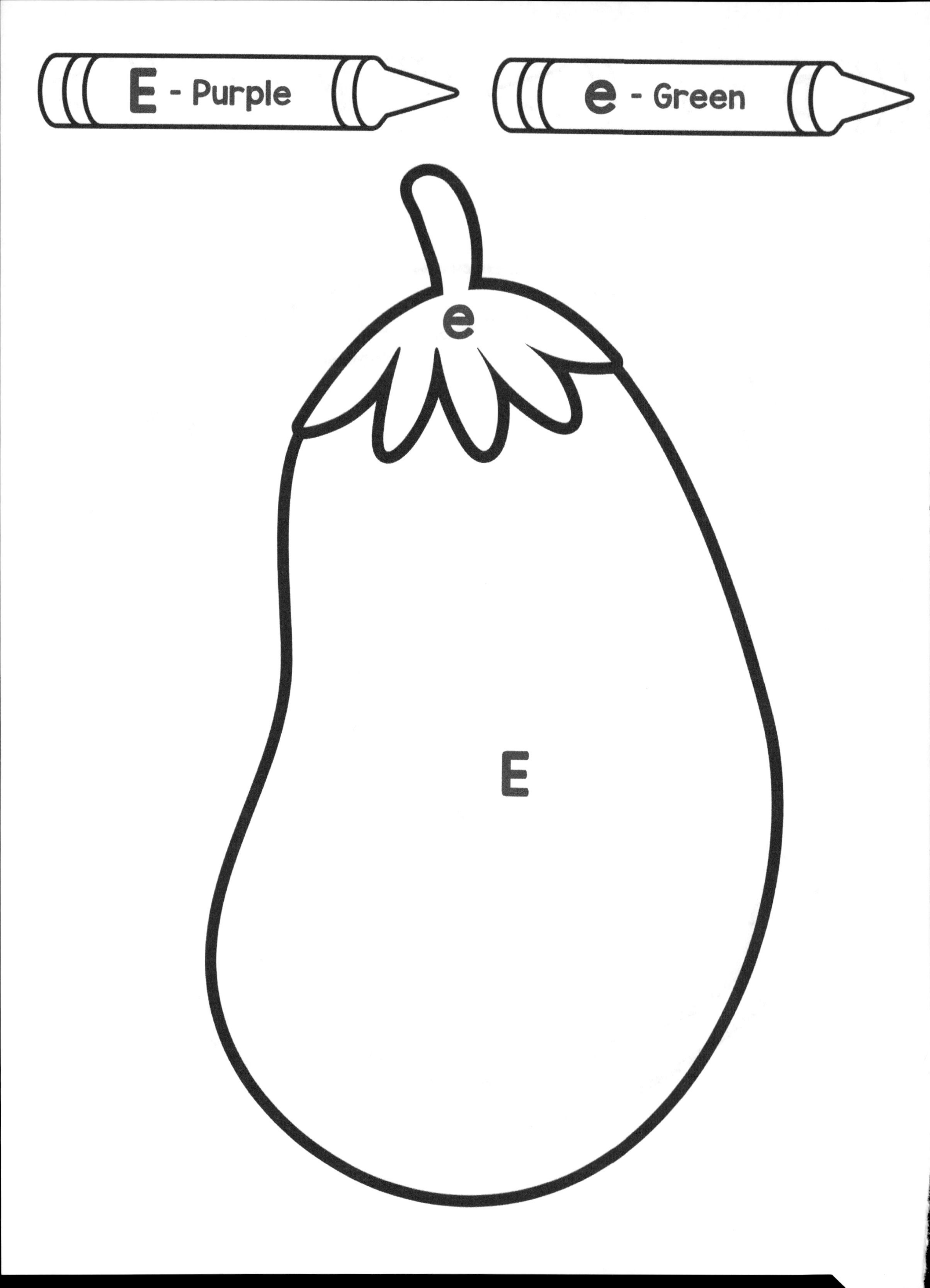
E - Purple
e - Green
e
E

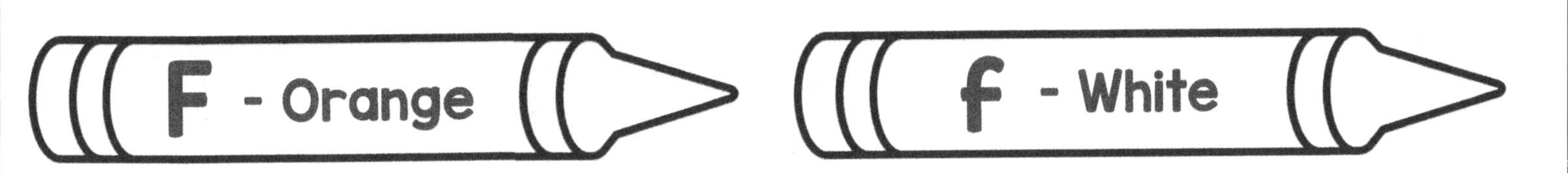
F - Orange
f - White

F
f
F
f
F
f

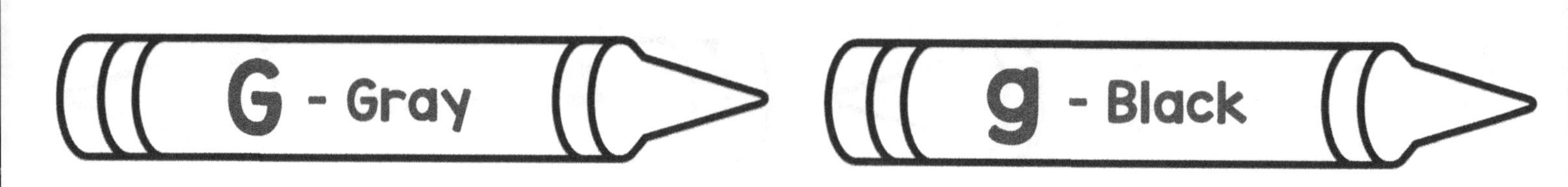
G - Gray
g - Black

g
G
G

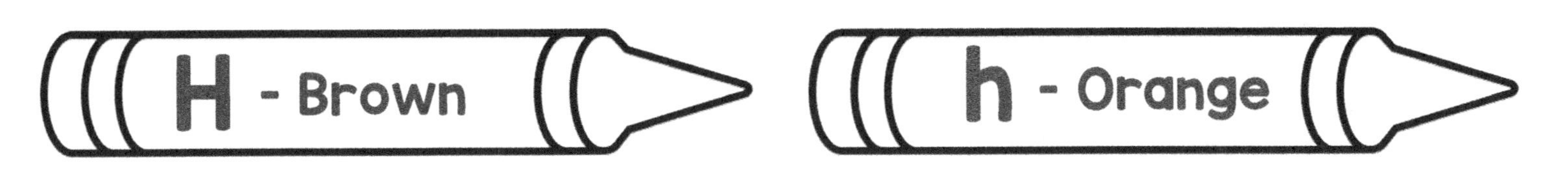
H - Brown
h - Orange

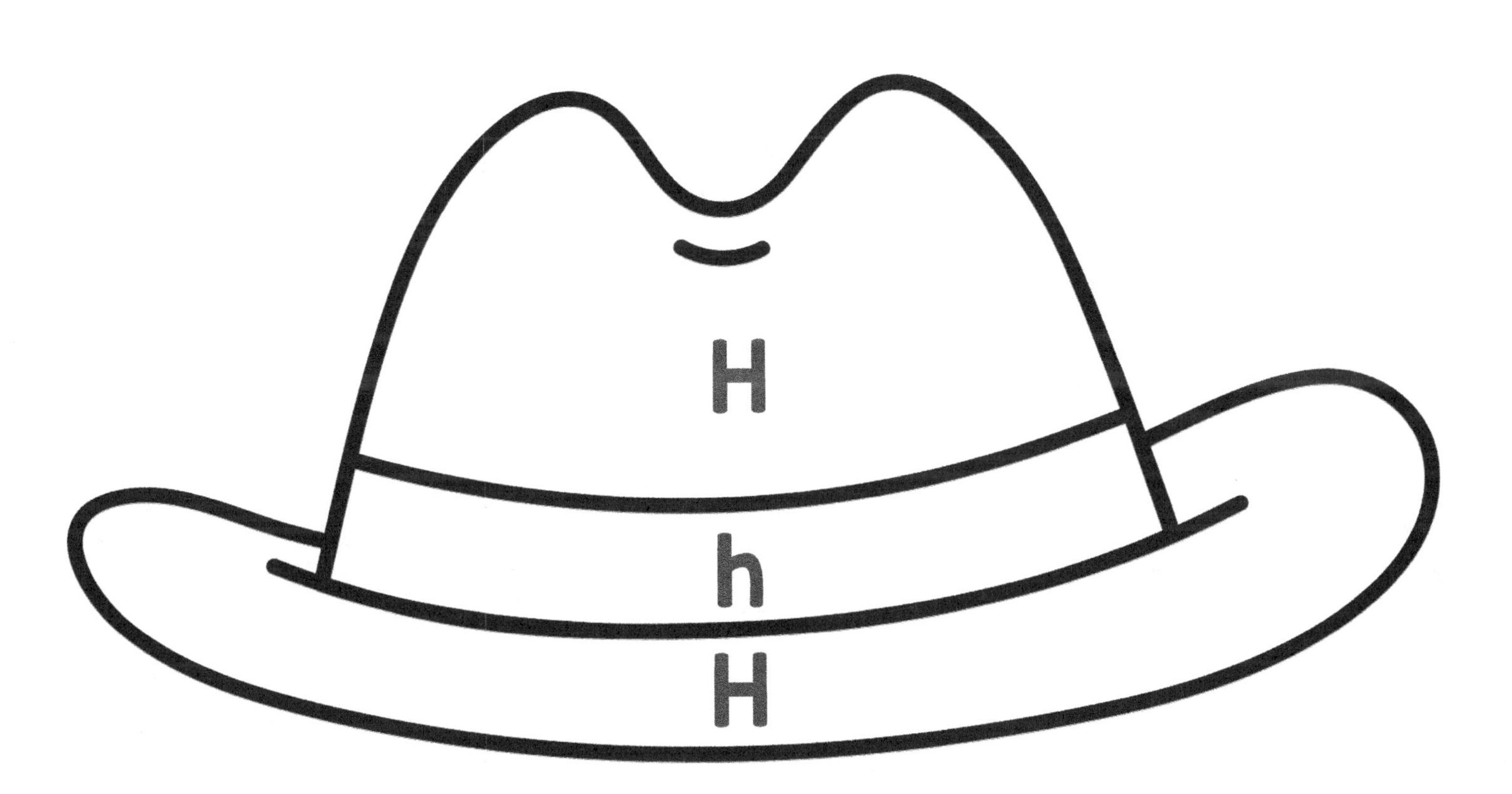
H
h
H

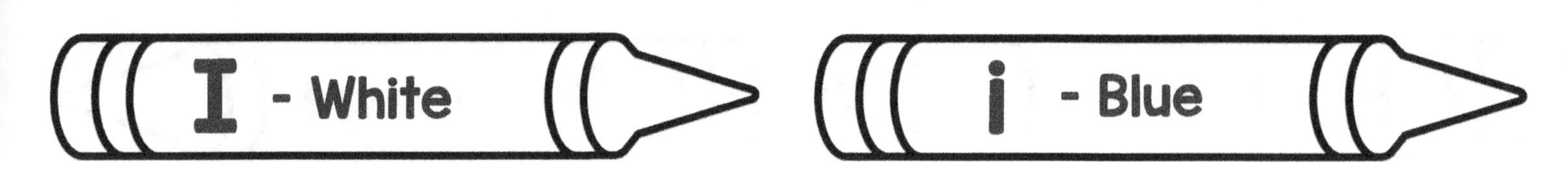
I - White
i - Blue

I
i
i

J - Red
j - Green
j
J
J
j
J
j
J
J

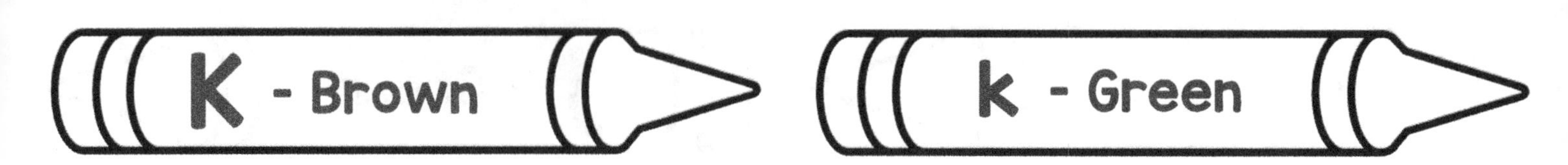
K - Brown
k - Green

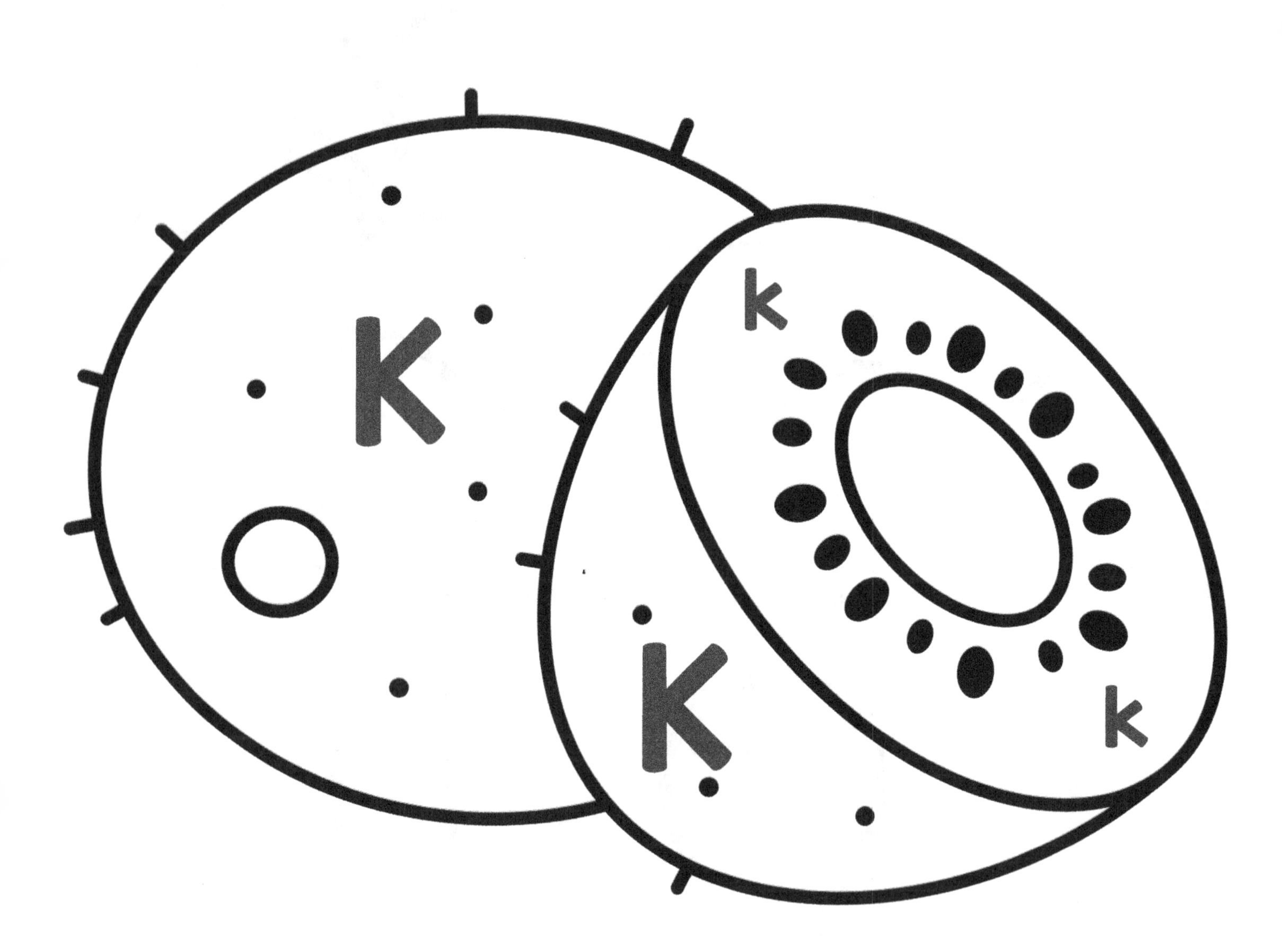
K
k
K
k

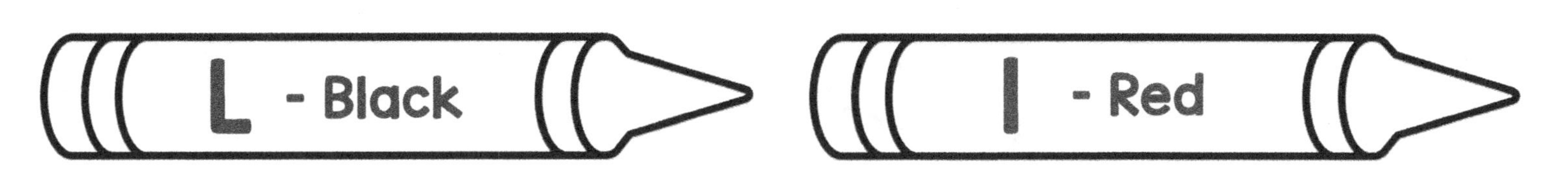
L - Black
l - Red

l
L
L
L
l
L
L
L
L
L
L
L
L

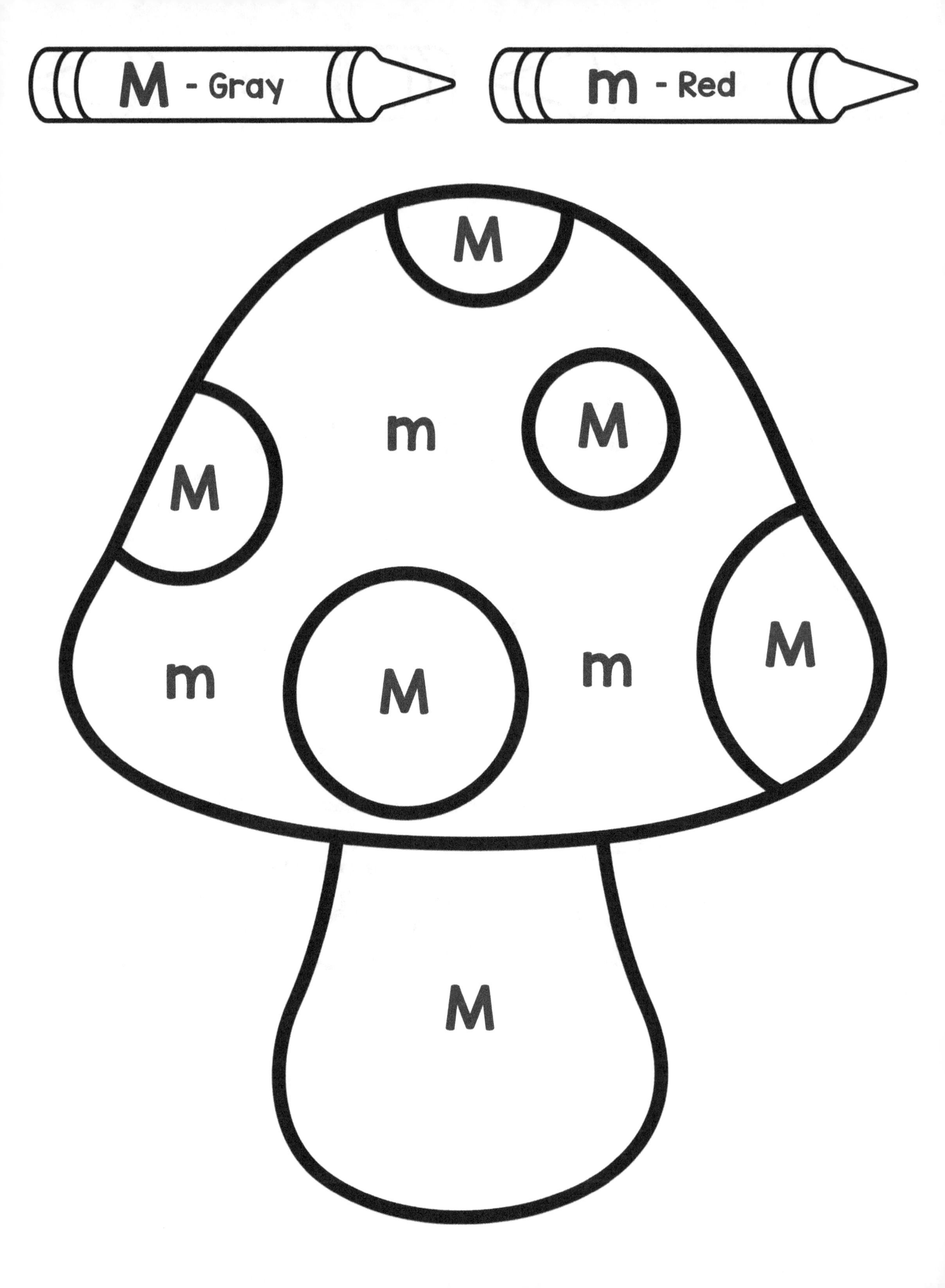
M - Gray
m - Red
M
m
M
M
m
M
m
M
M

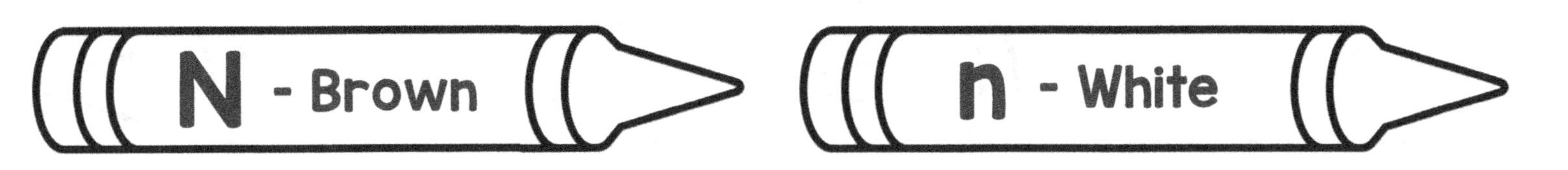
N - Brown
n - White

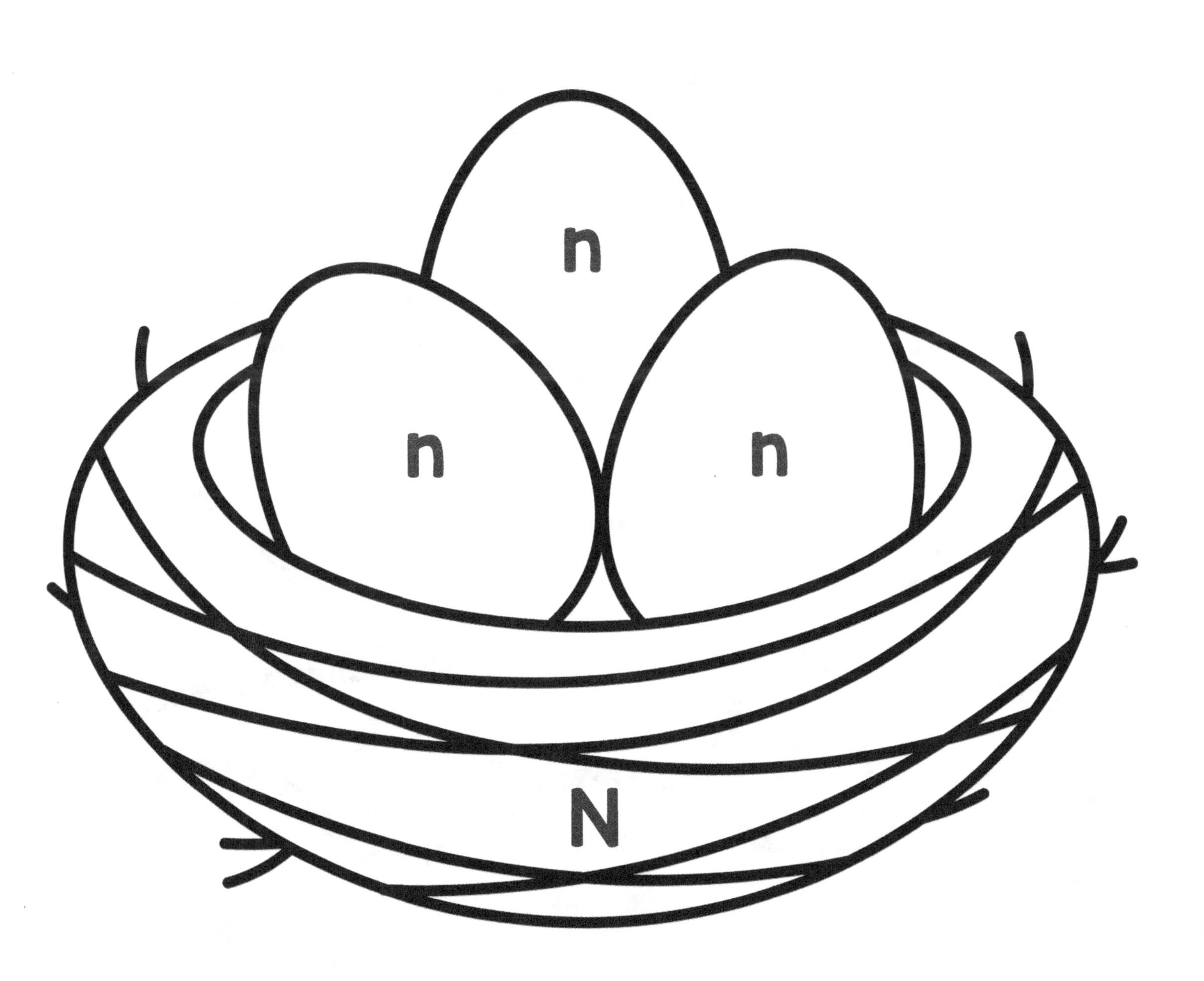
n
n
n
N

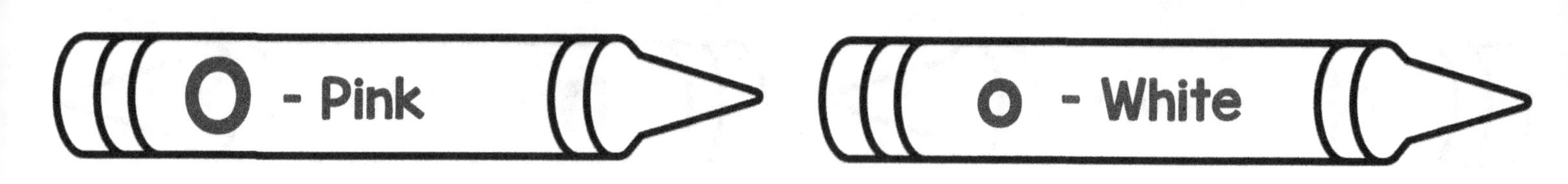
O - Pink
o - White

O
o
O
O
O

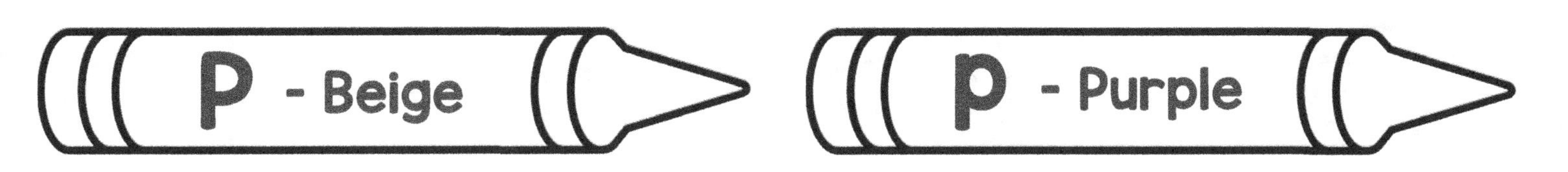
P - Beige
p - Purple

P
p

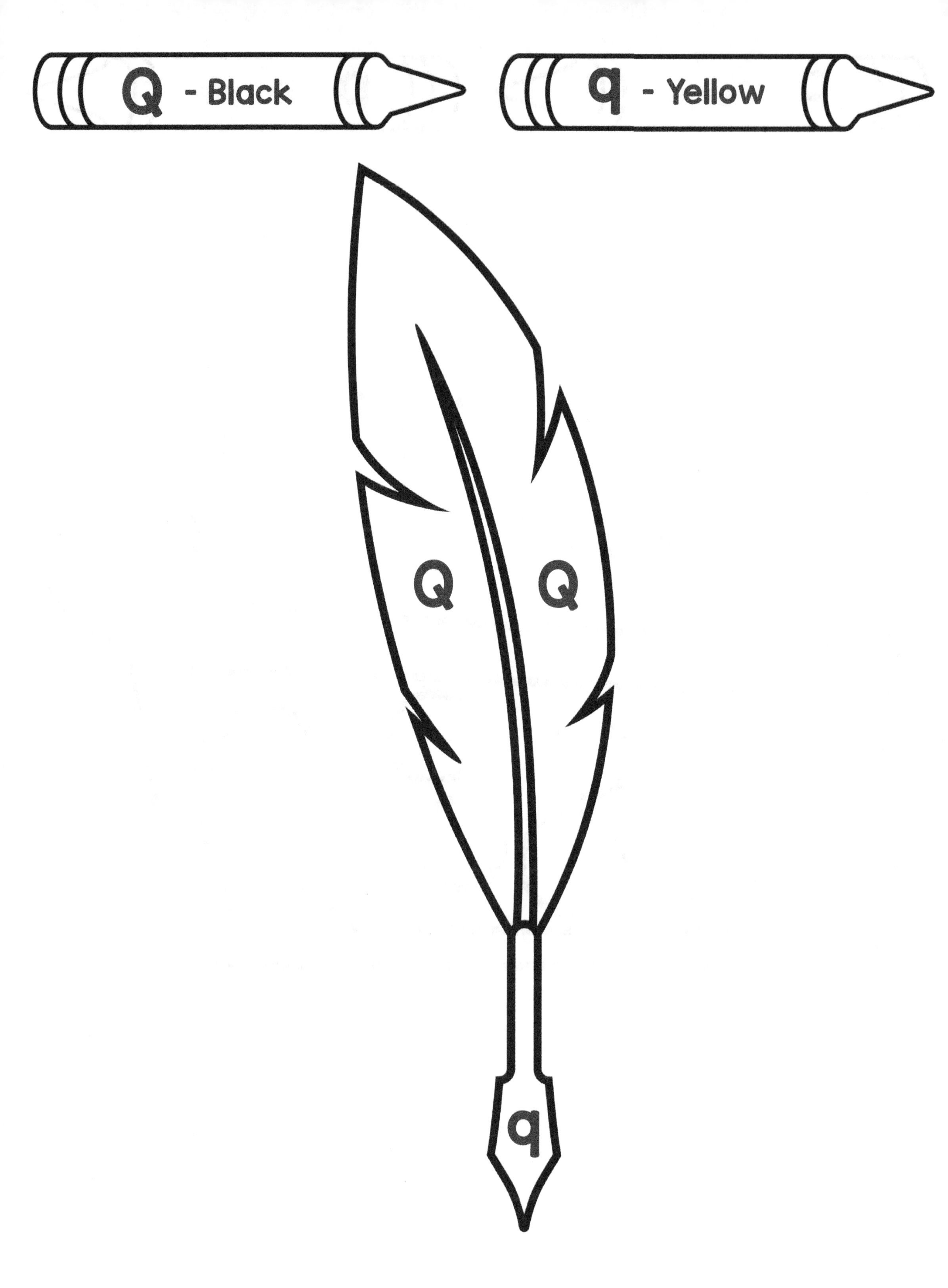
Q - Black
q - Yellow
Q
Q
q

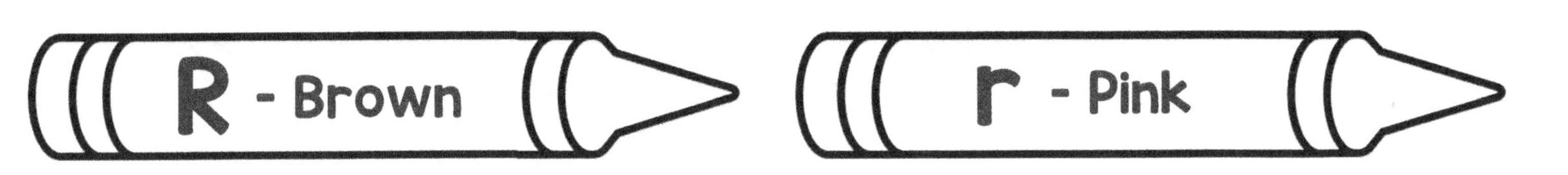
R - Brown
r - Pink

r
r
R
R
R
R
R
R

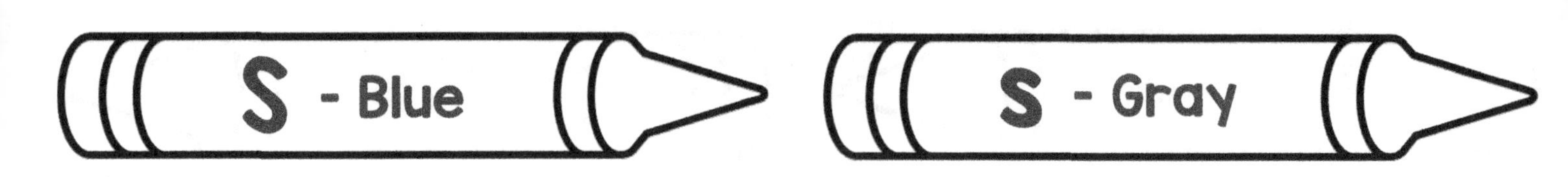
S - Blue
s - Gray

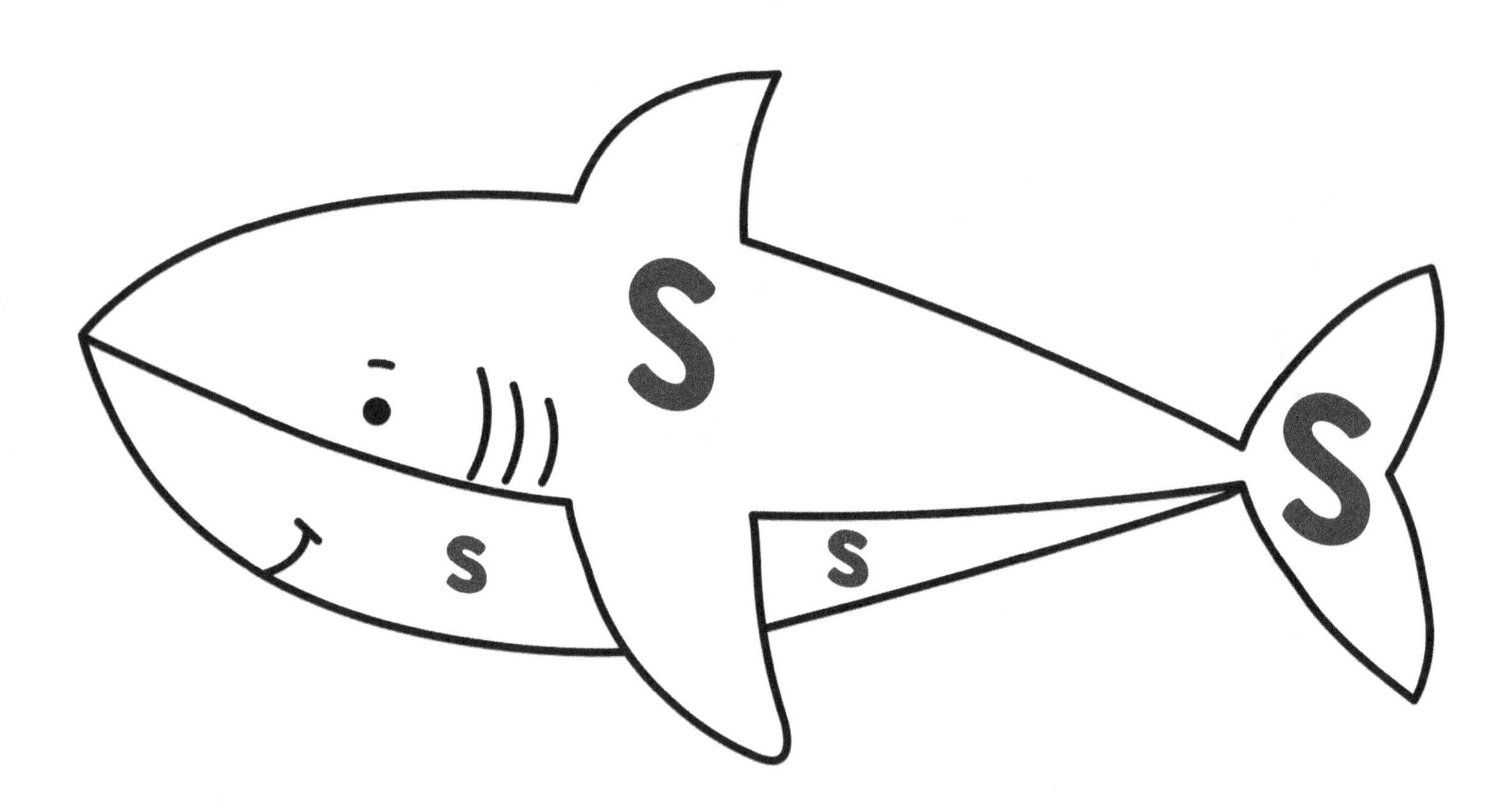
S
S
s
s

T - Green
t - Brown
T
T
T
t

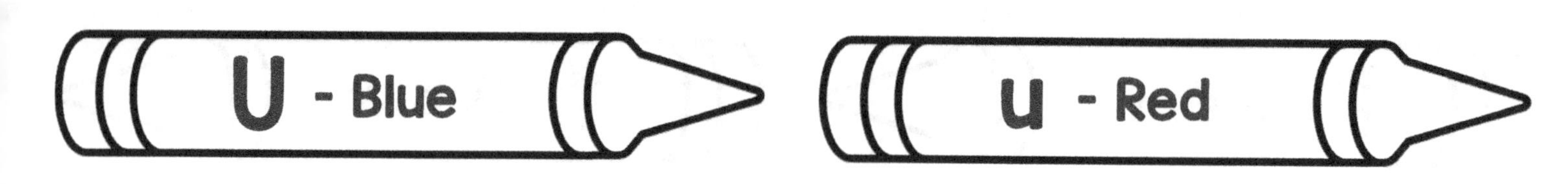
U - Blue
u - Red

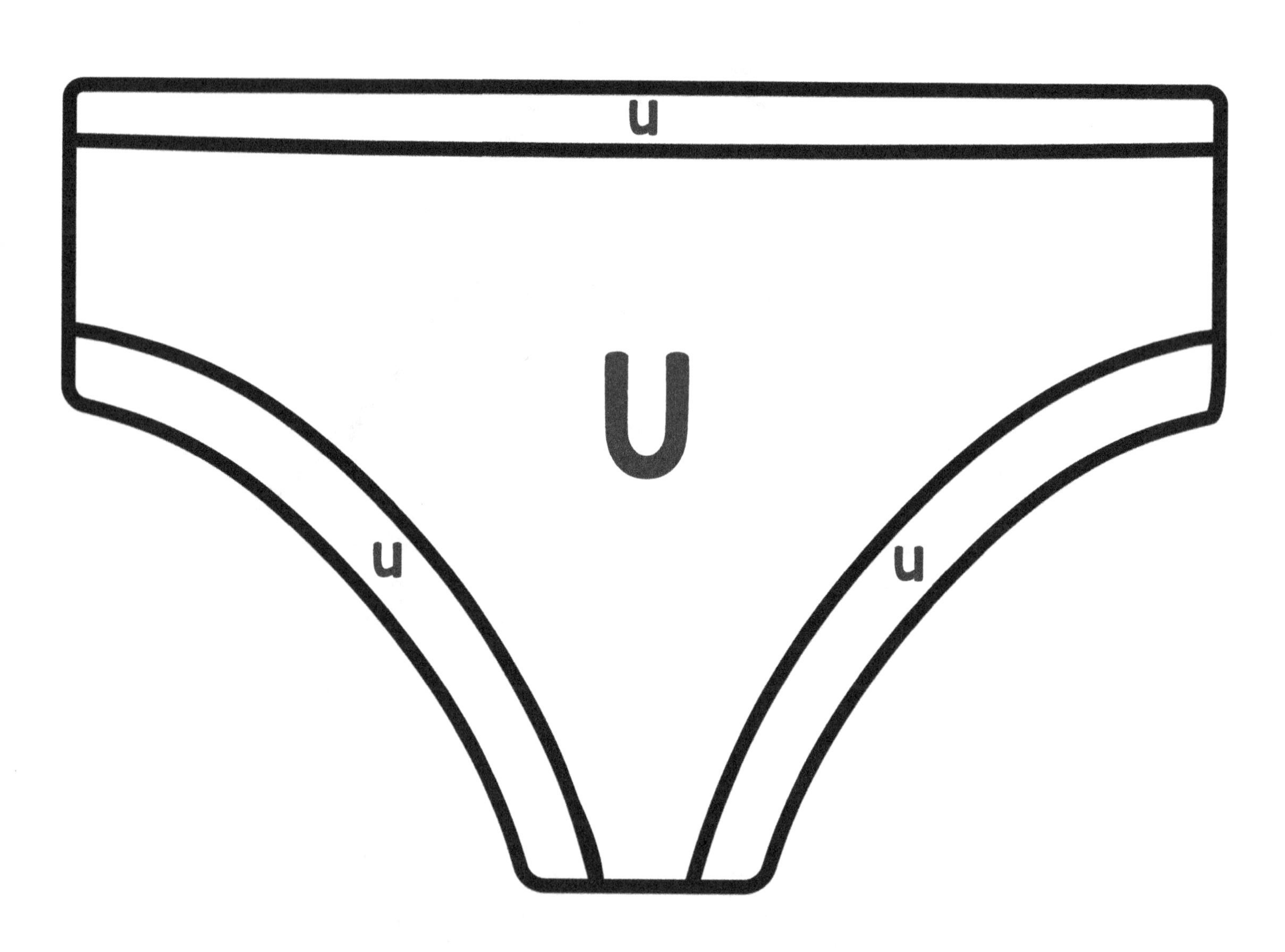
u
U
u
u

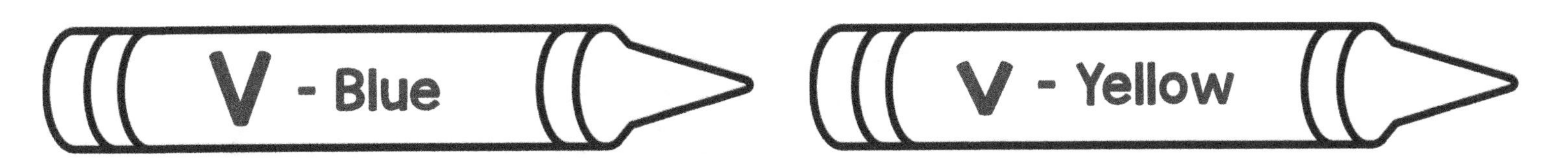
V - Blue
v - Yellow

v
V
V
v
V
v

W - Yellow
w - Orange
W
w

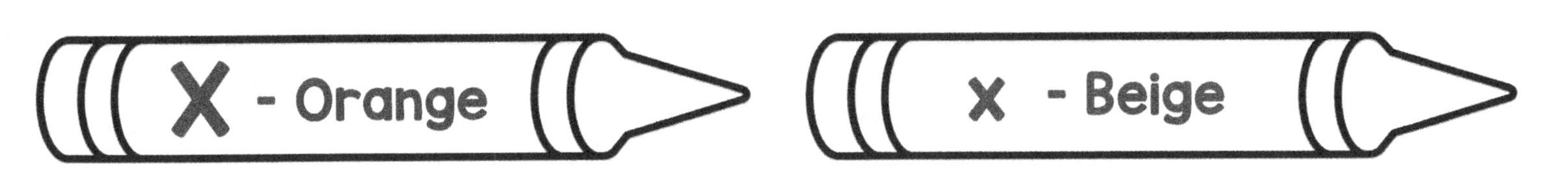
X - Orange
x - Beige

x
X
x
x
x
X
x
X
x
x
x
x
x

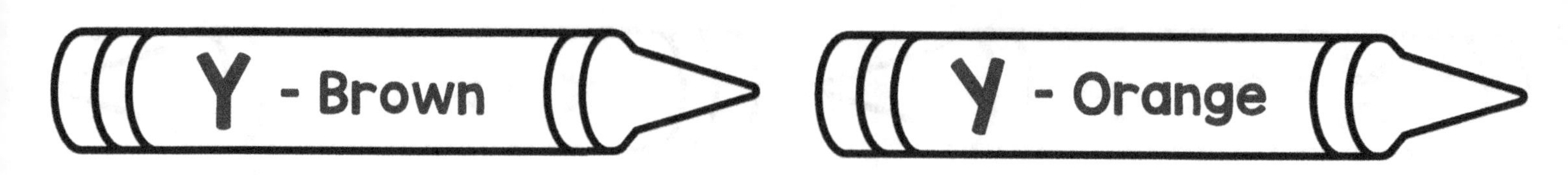
Y - Brown
Y - Orange

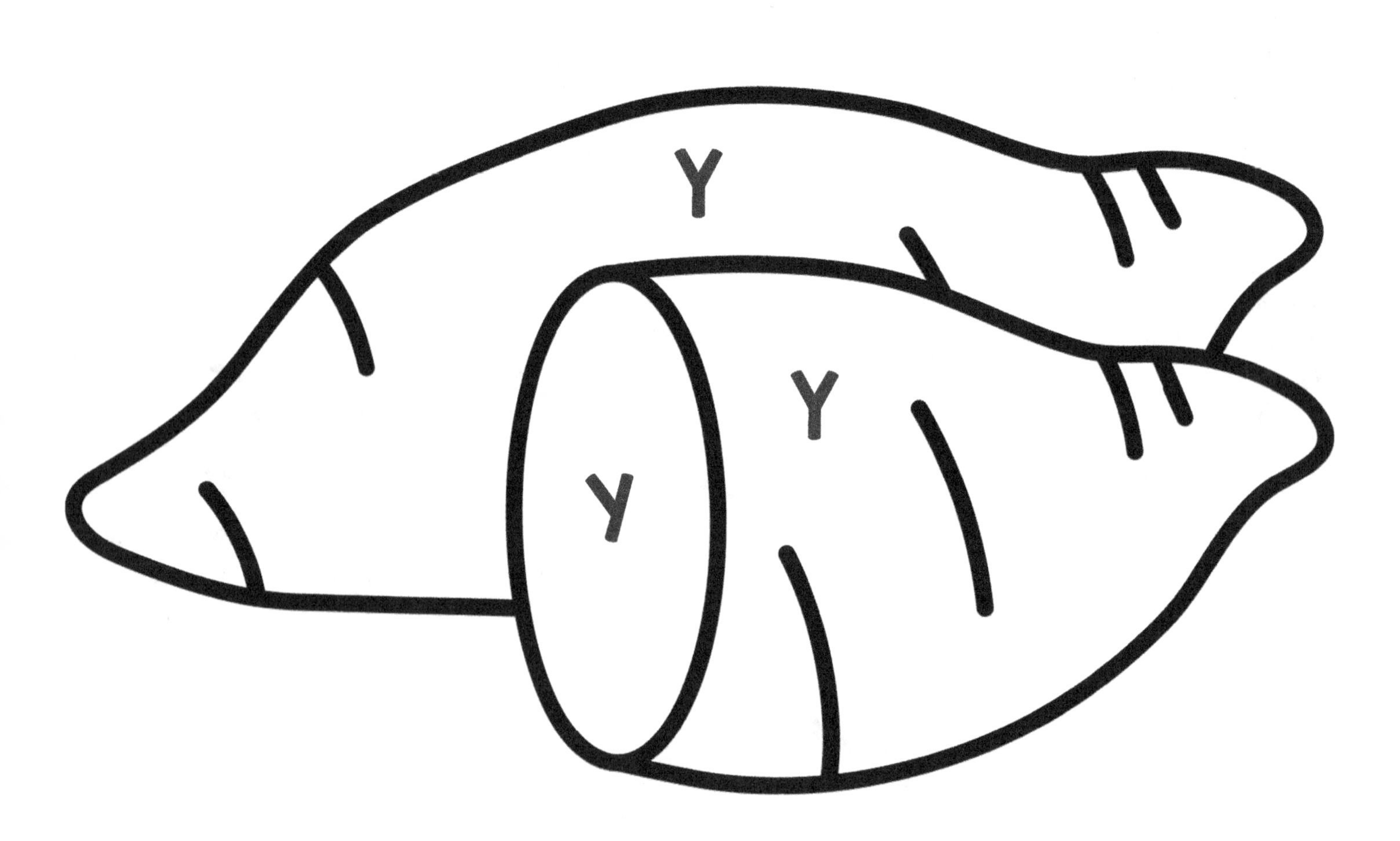
Y
Y
Y

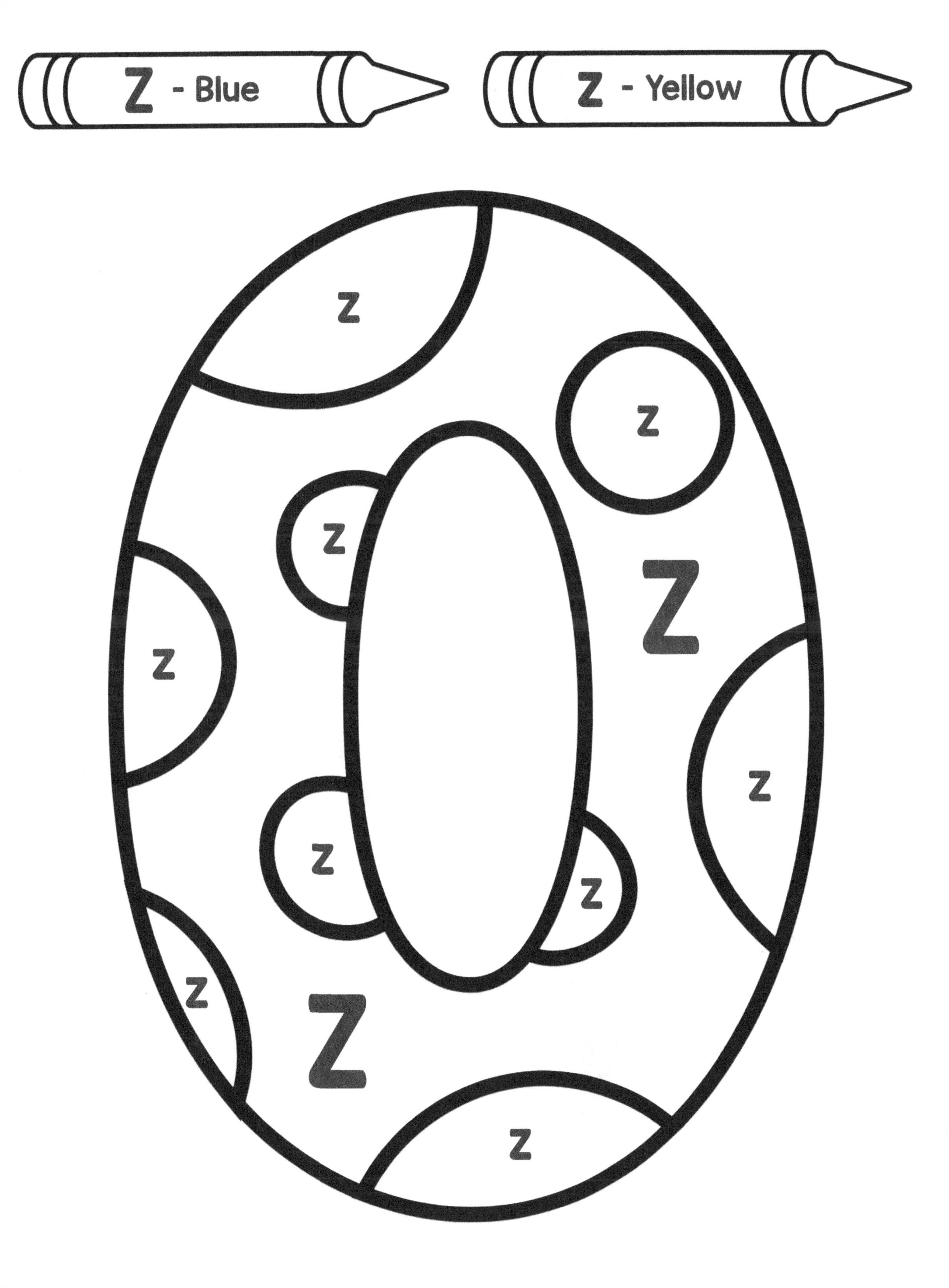

Z - Blue
z - Yellow
z
z
z
Z
z
z
z
z
z
Z
z

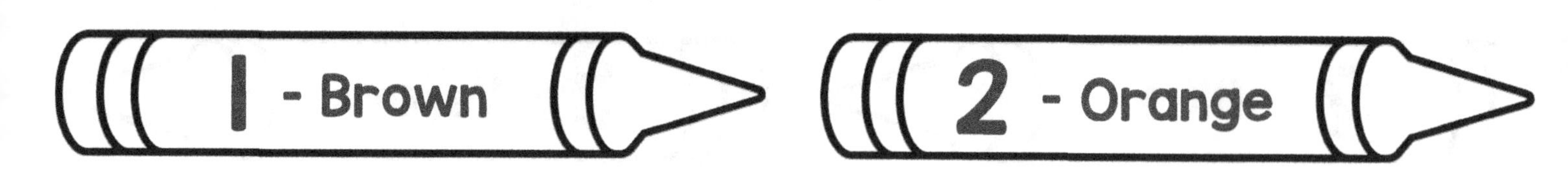
1 - Brown
2 - Orange

2
1
2
2

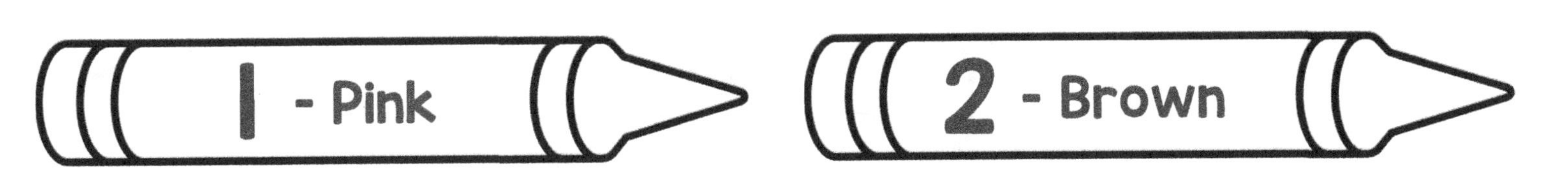
1 - Pink
2 - Brown

1
1
2
1
2
2
1
1
2
2

1 - Pink
2 - Orange
1
2
1
1
1
1
2
2

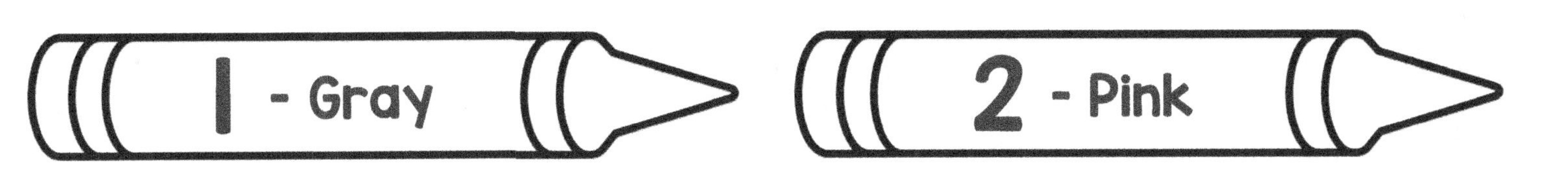
1 - Gray
2 - Pink

1
1
2
1
2
1
1
1
1
1
1

1 - Red
2 - Brown
3 - Green
2
3
1

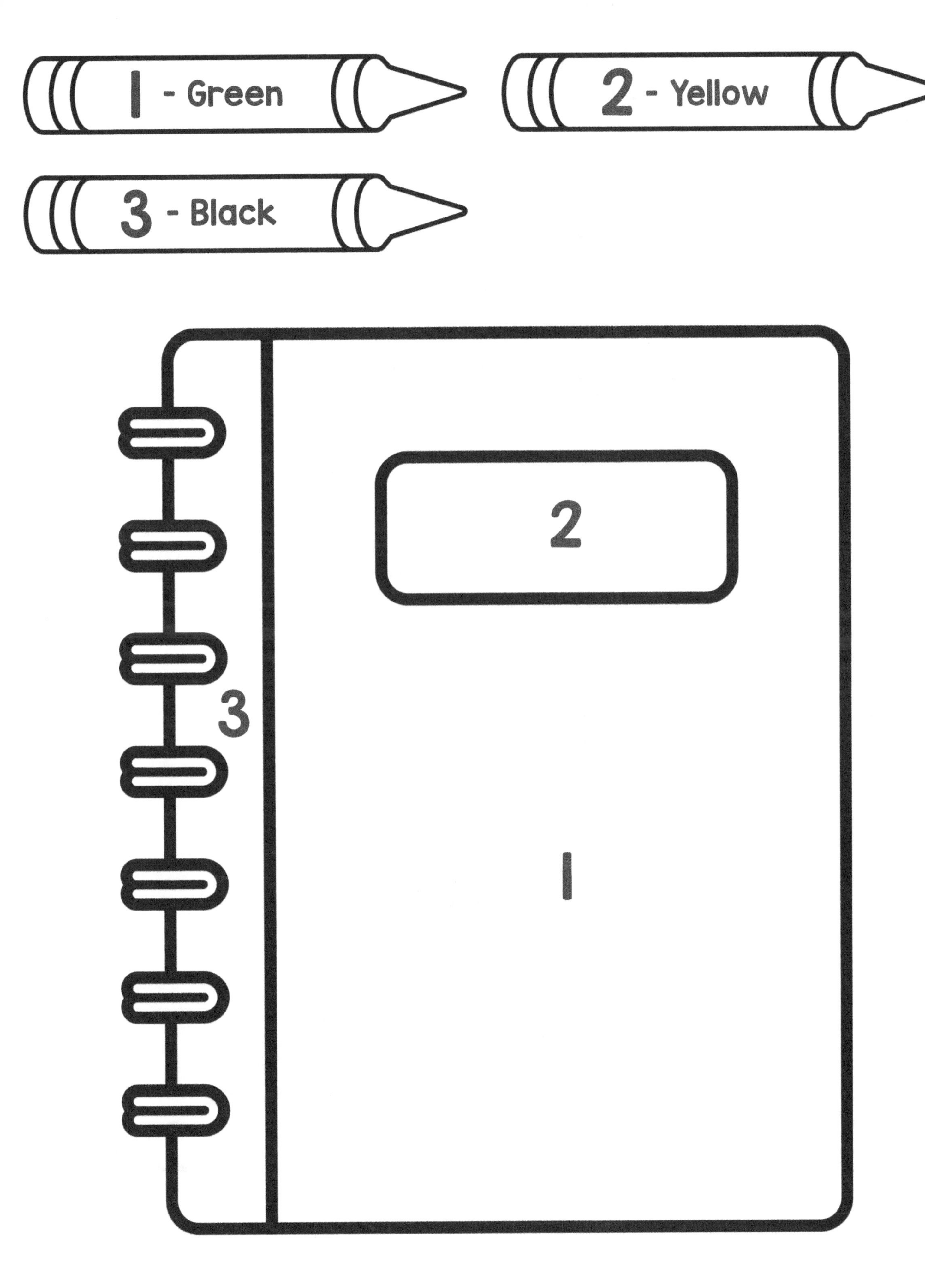
1 - Green
2 - Yellow
3 - Black
2
3
1

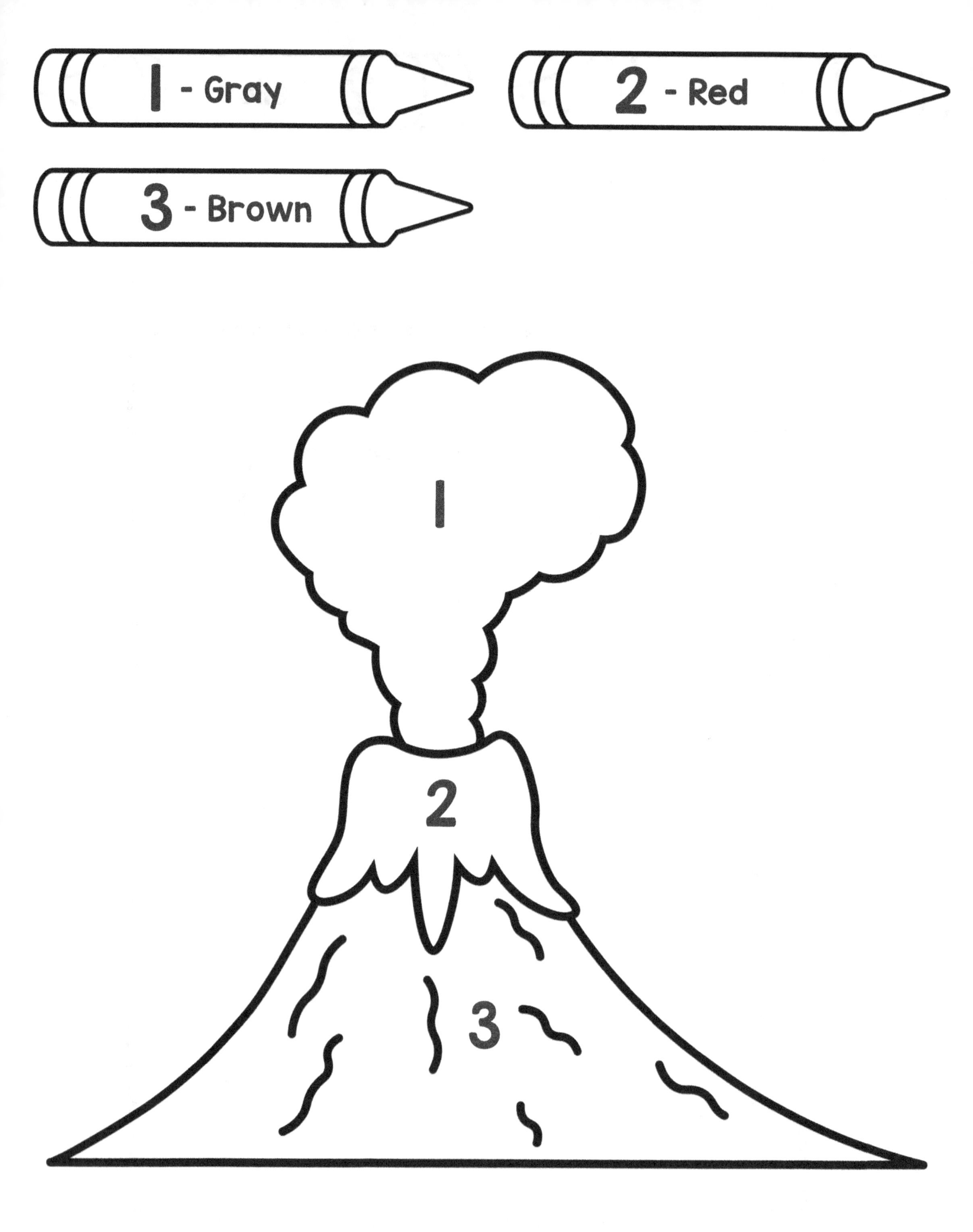
1 - Gray
2 - Red
3 - Brown
1
2
3

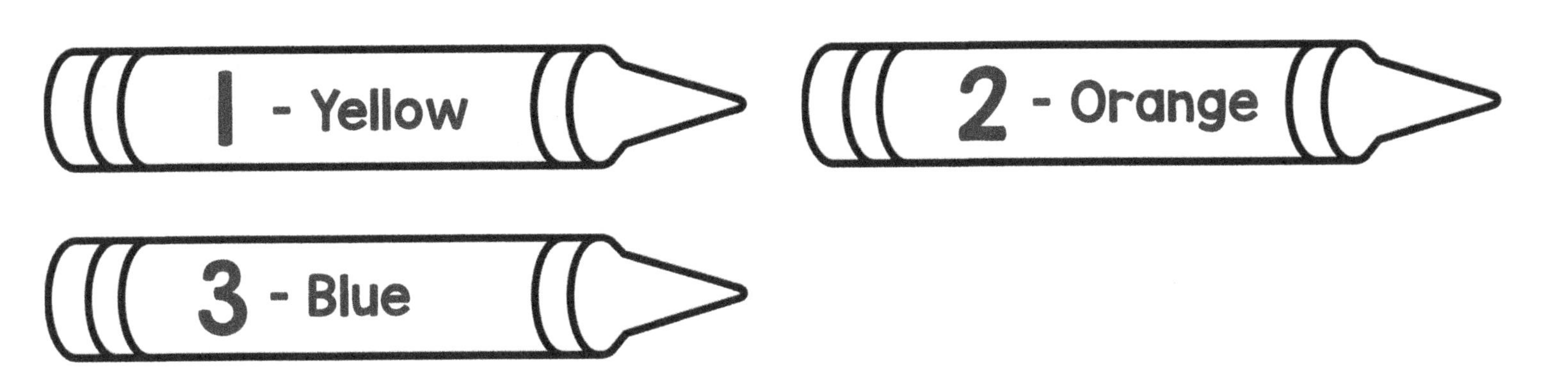
1 - Yellow
2 - Orange
3 - Blue

2
1
1
1
1
3
3
3

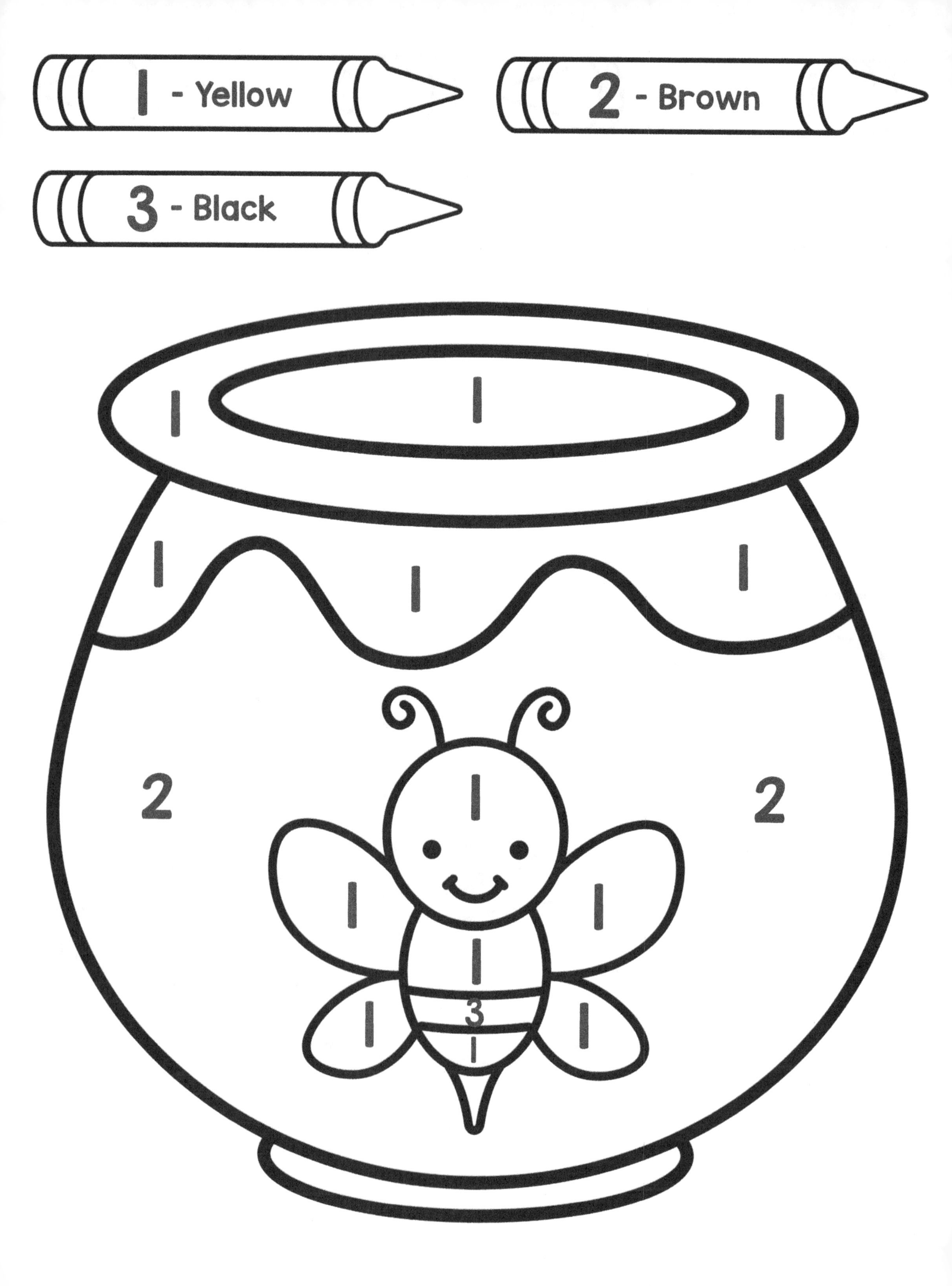
1 - Yellow
2 - Brown
3 - Black
1
1
1
1
1
1
2
1
2
1
1
1
1
3
1
1

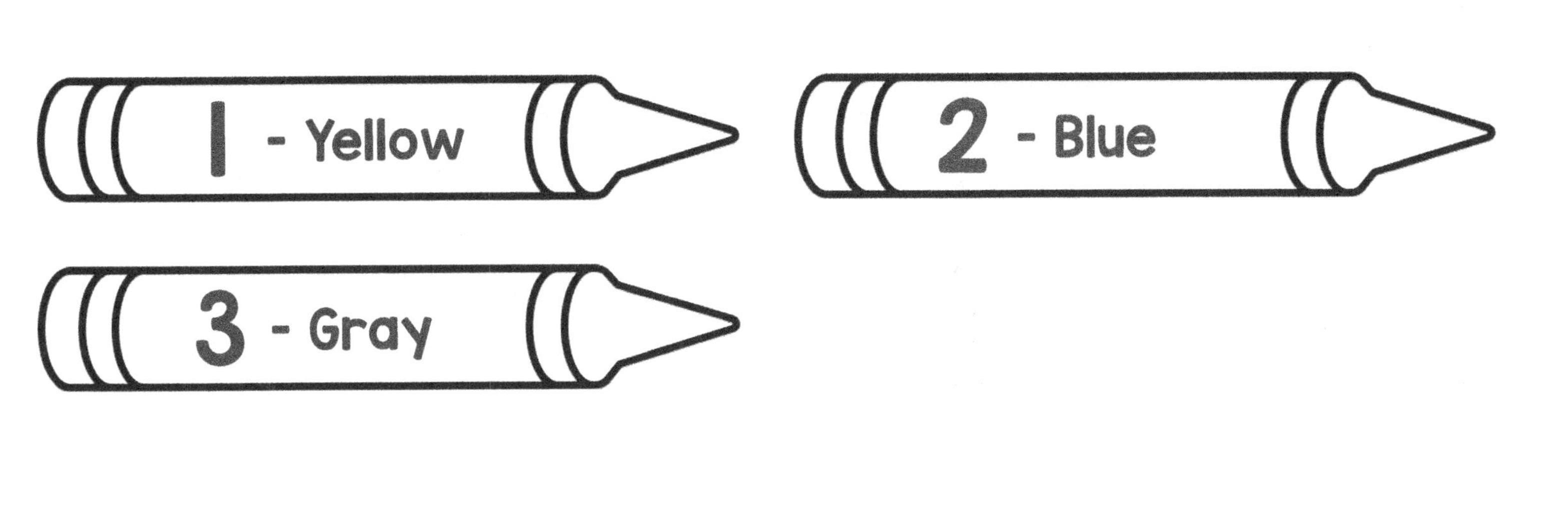
1 - Yellow
2 - Blue
3 - Gray

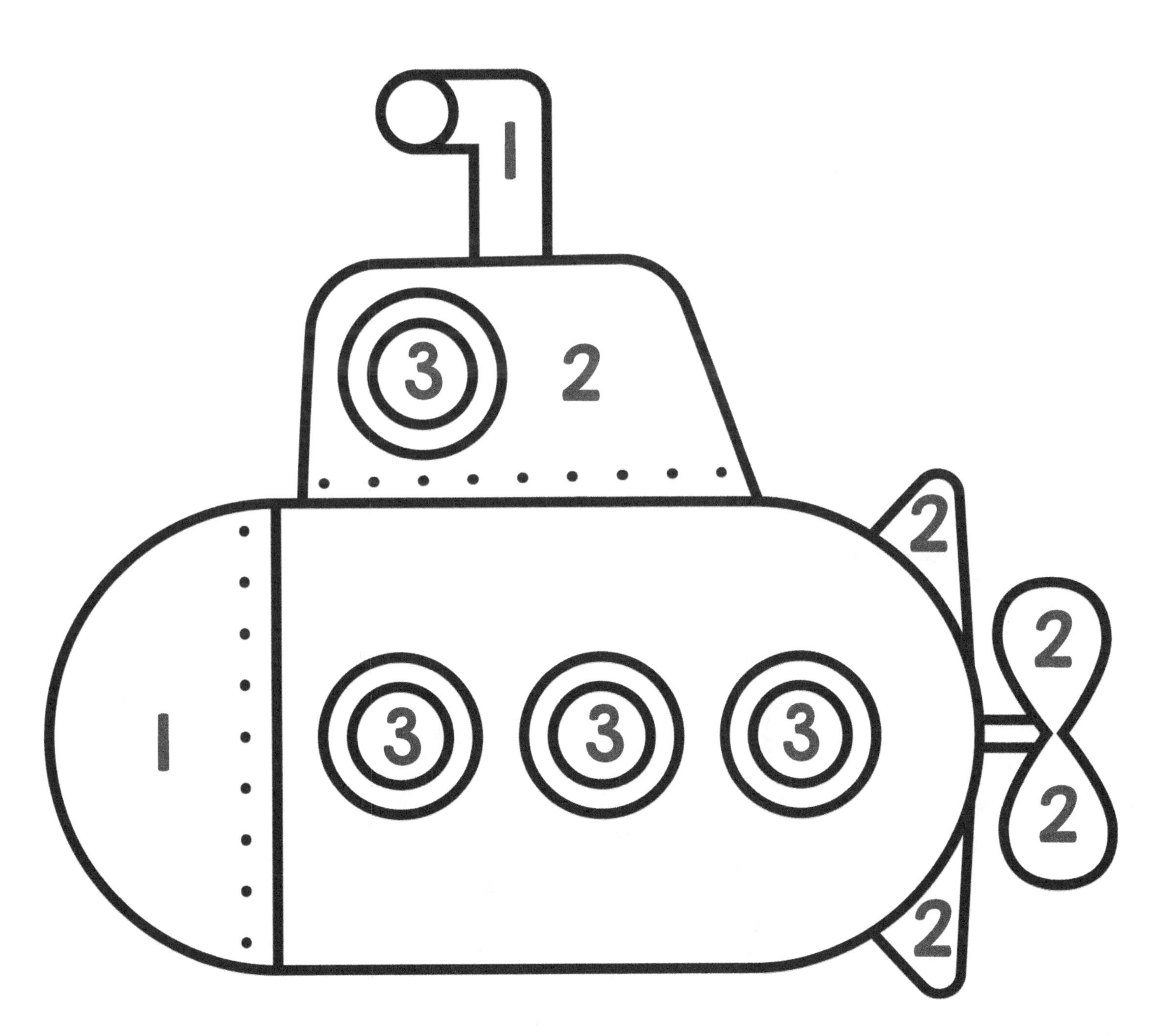
1
3
2
2
2
1
3
3
3
2
2

1 - Gray
2 - Brown
3 - Black
3
3
1
2
2
2
2
1
1
1
1
1
3
3
3
3

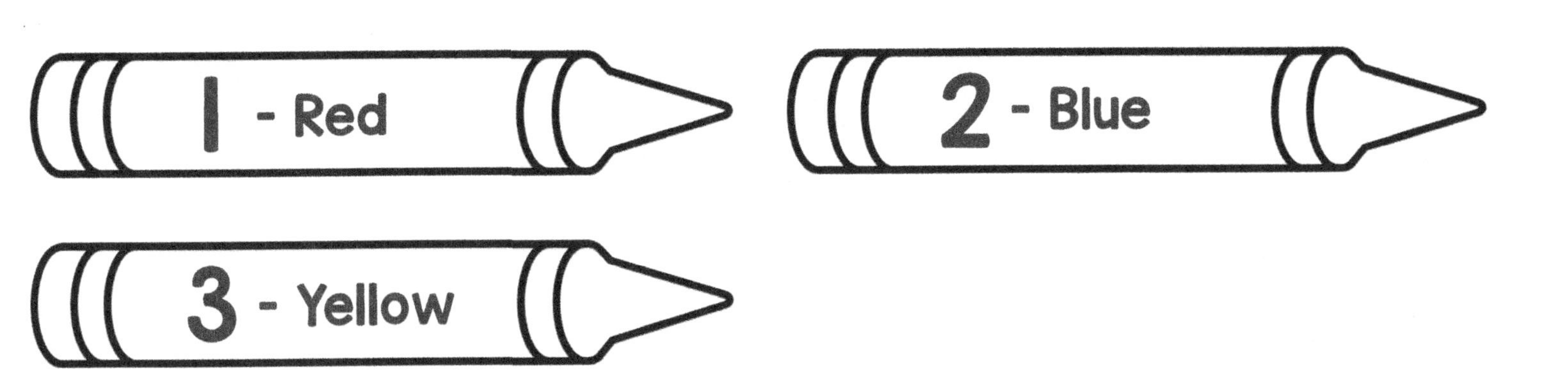
1 - Red
2 - Blue
3 - Yellow

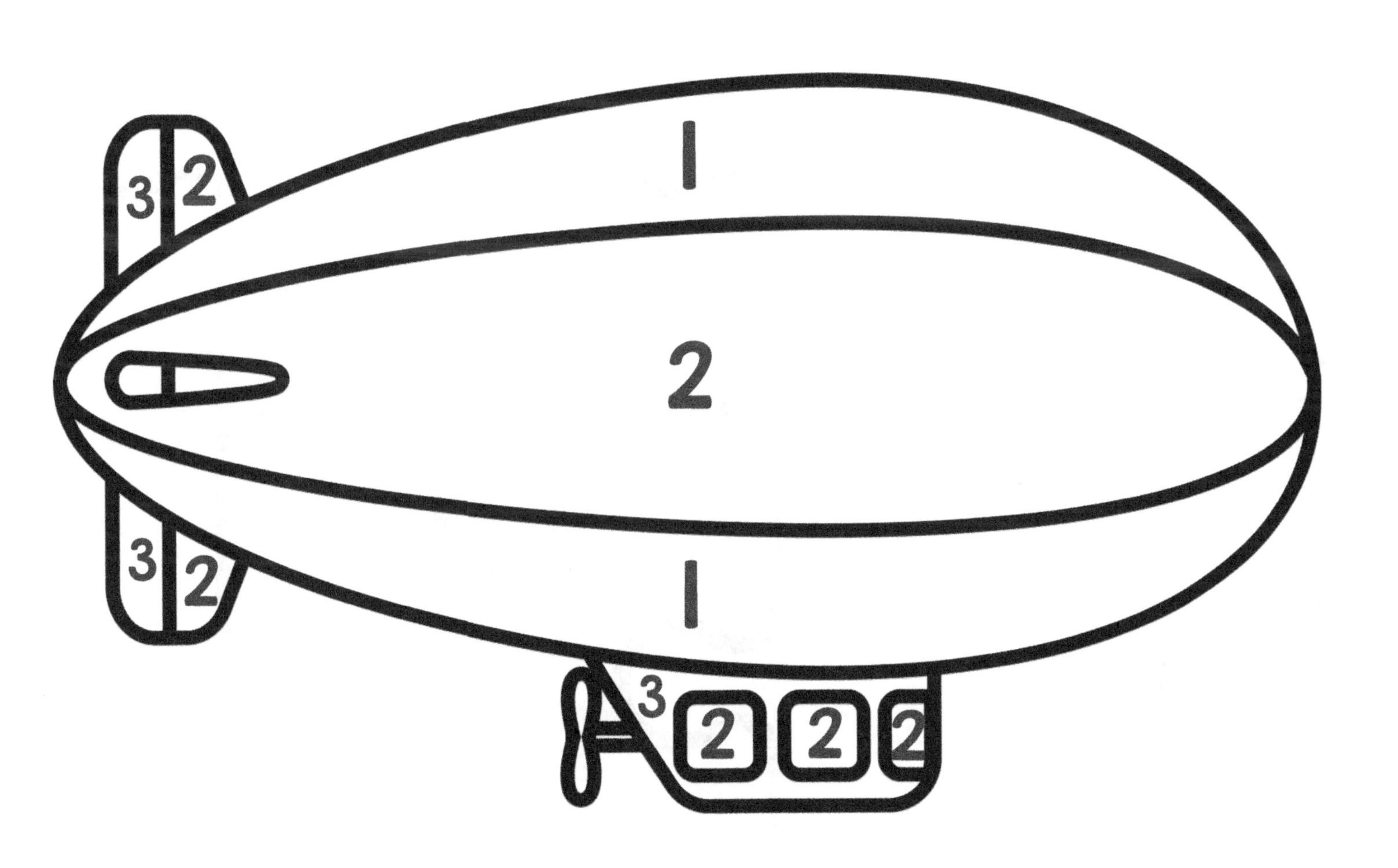
1
3
2
2
3
2
1
3
2
2
2

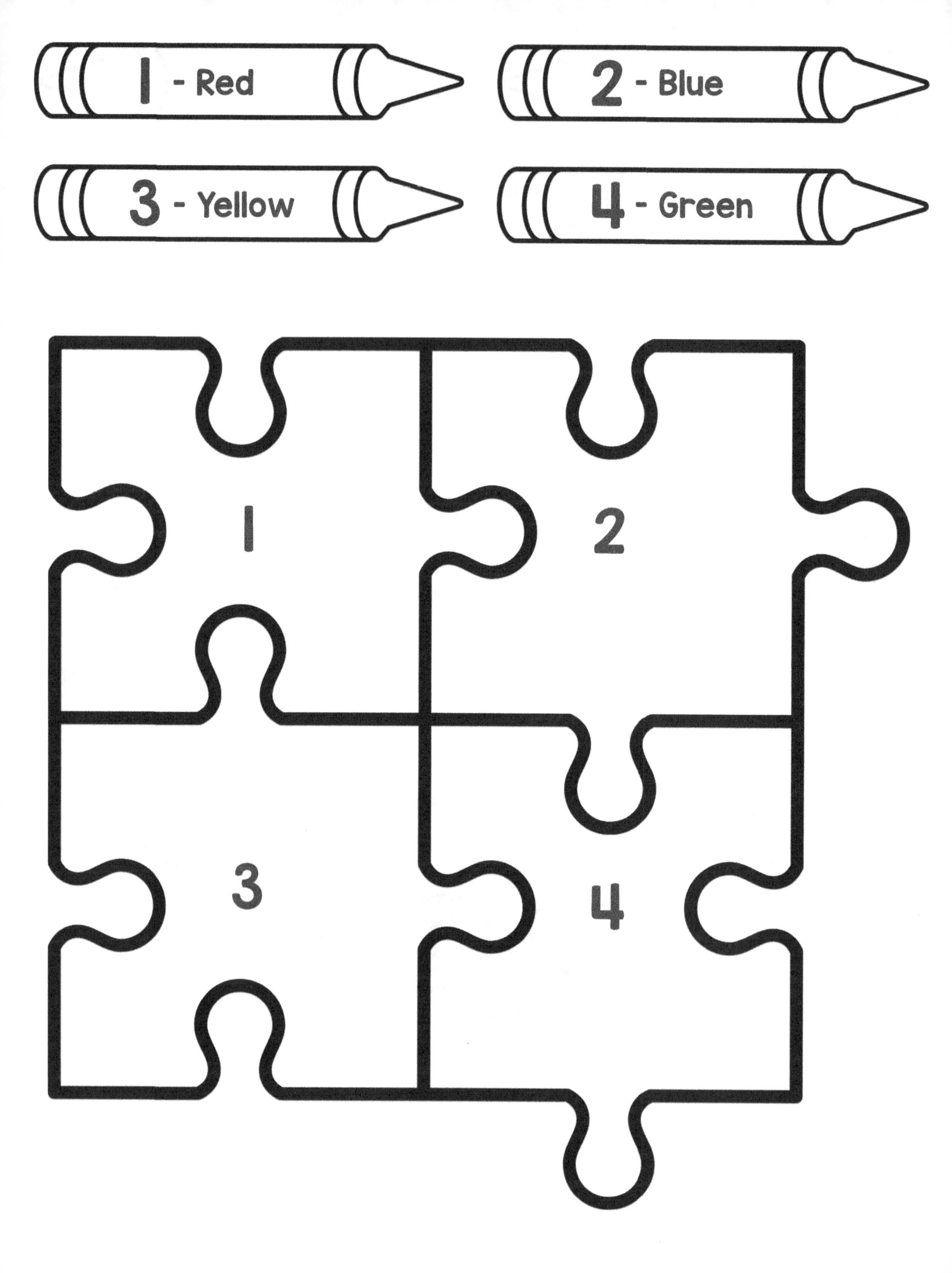
1 - Red
2 - Blue
3 - Yellow
4 - Green
1
2
3
4

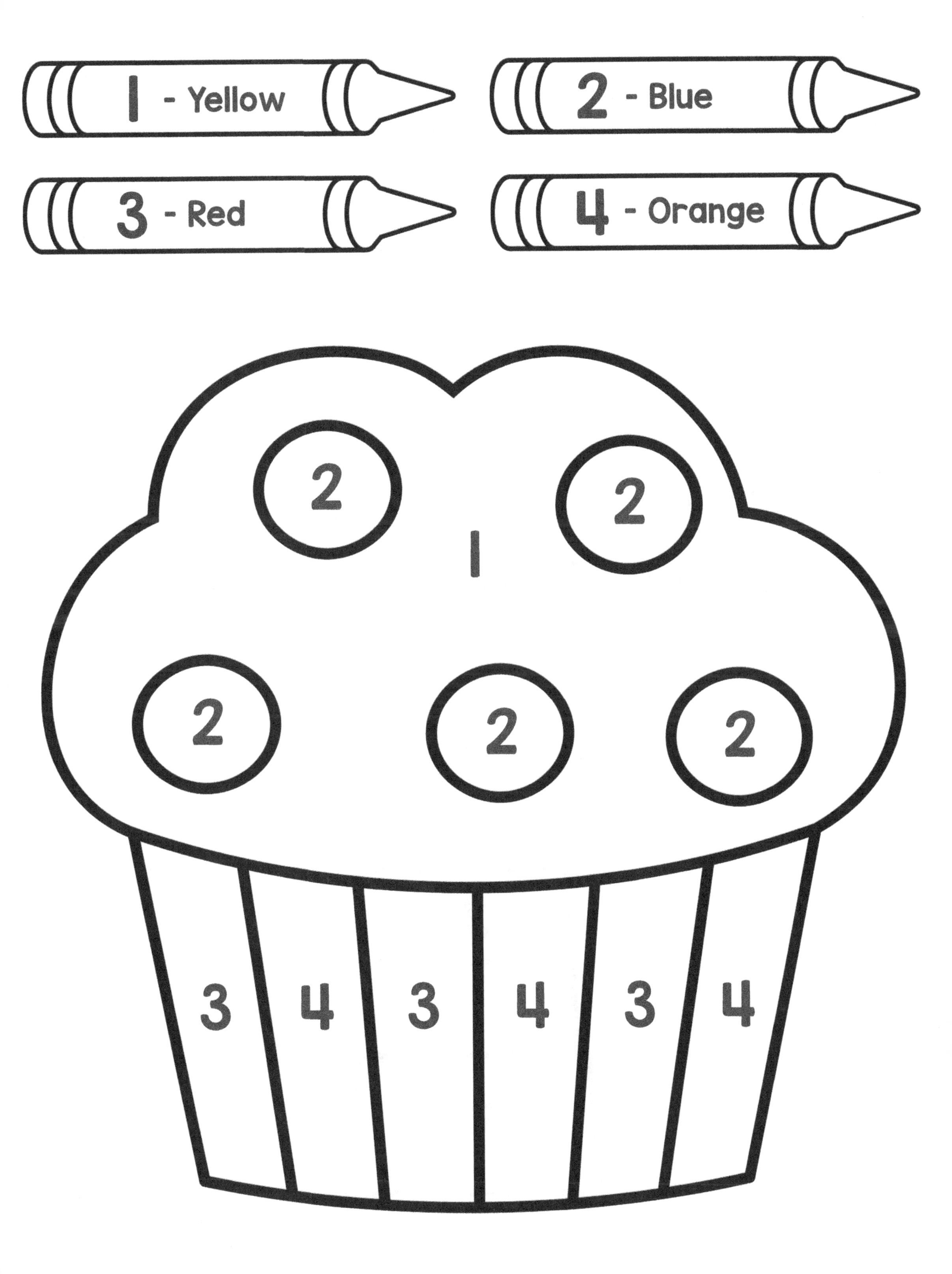
1 - Yellow
2 - Blue
3 - Red
4 - Orange
2
2
1
2
2
2
3
4
3
4
3
4

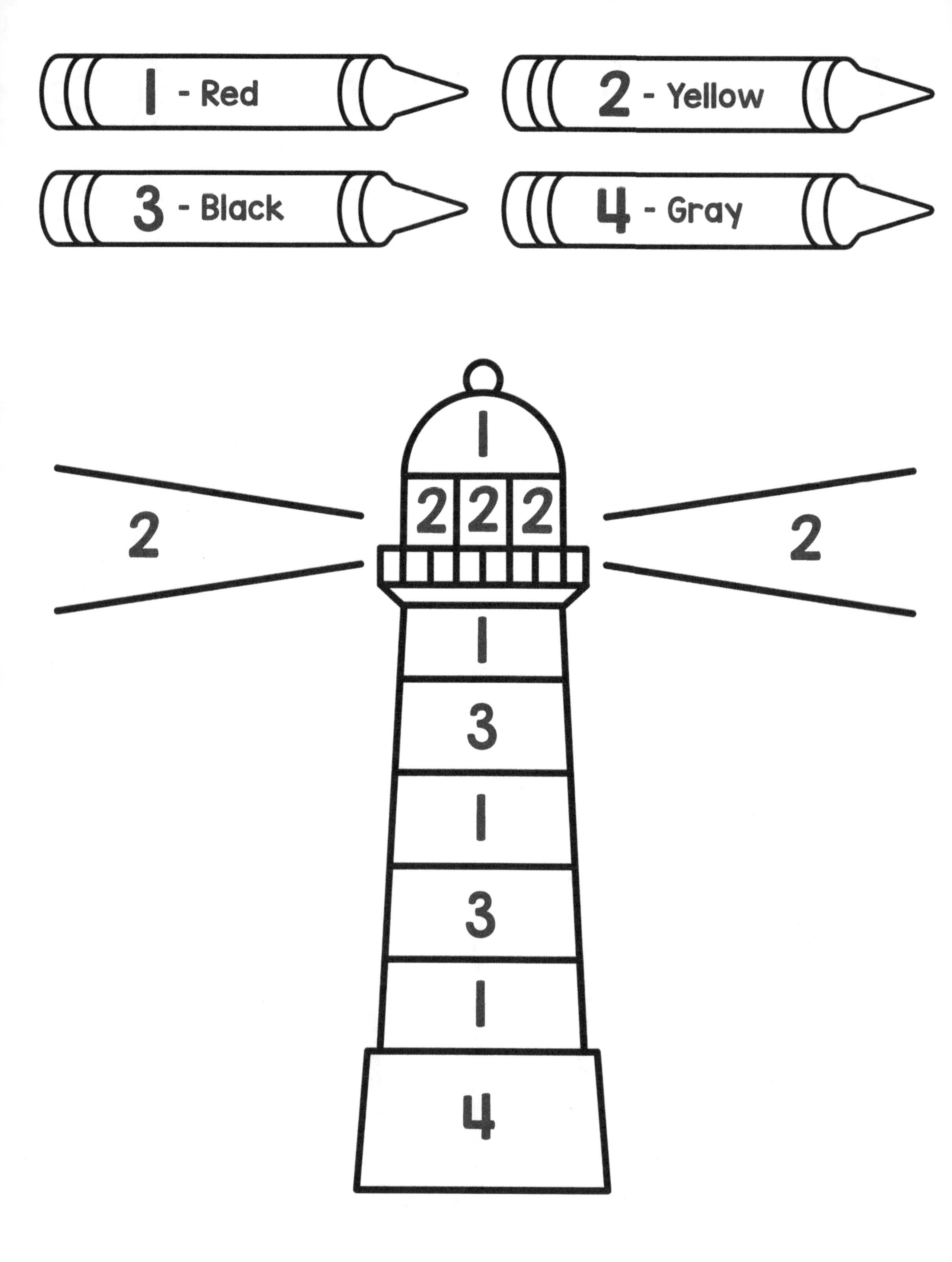
1 - Red
2 - Yellow
3 - Black
4 - Gray
1
2
2
2
2
2
1
3
1
3
1
4

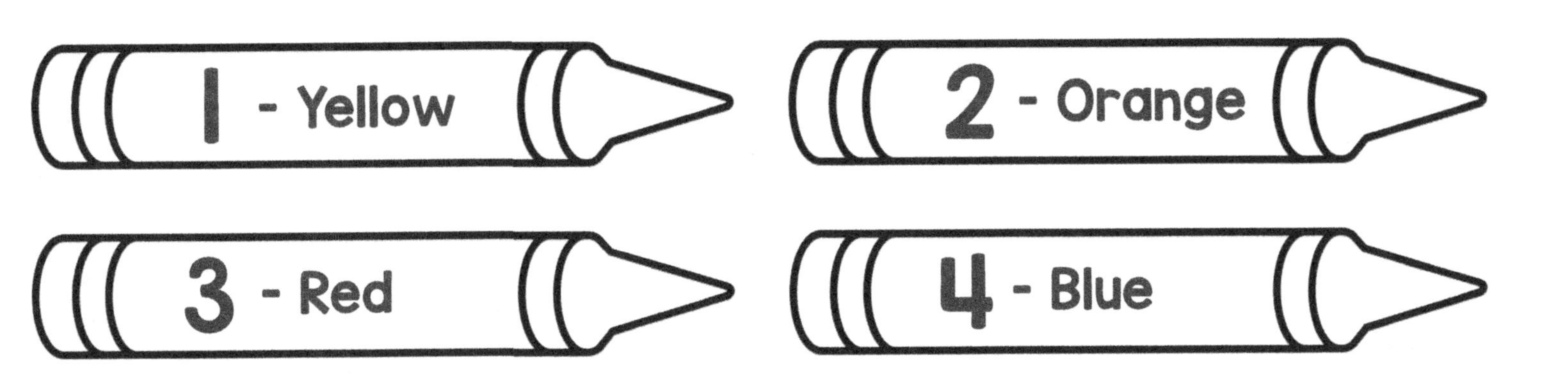
1 - Yellow
2 - Orange
3 - Red
4 - Blue

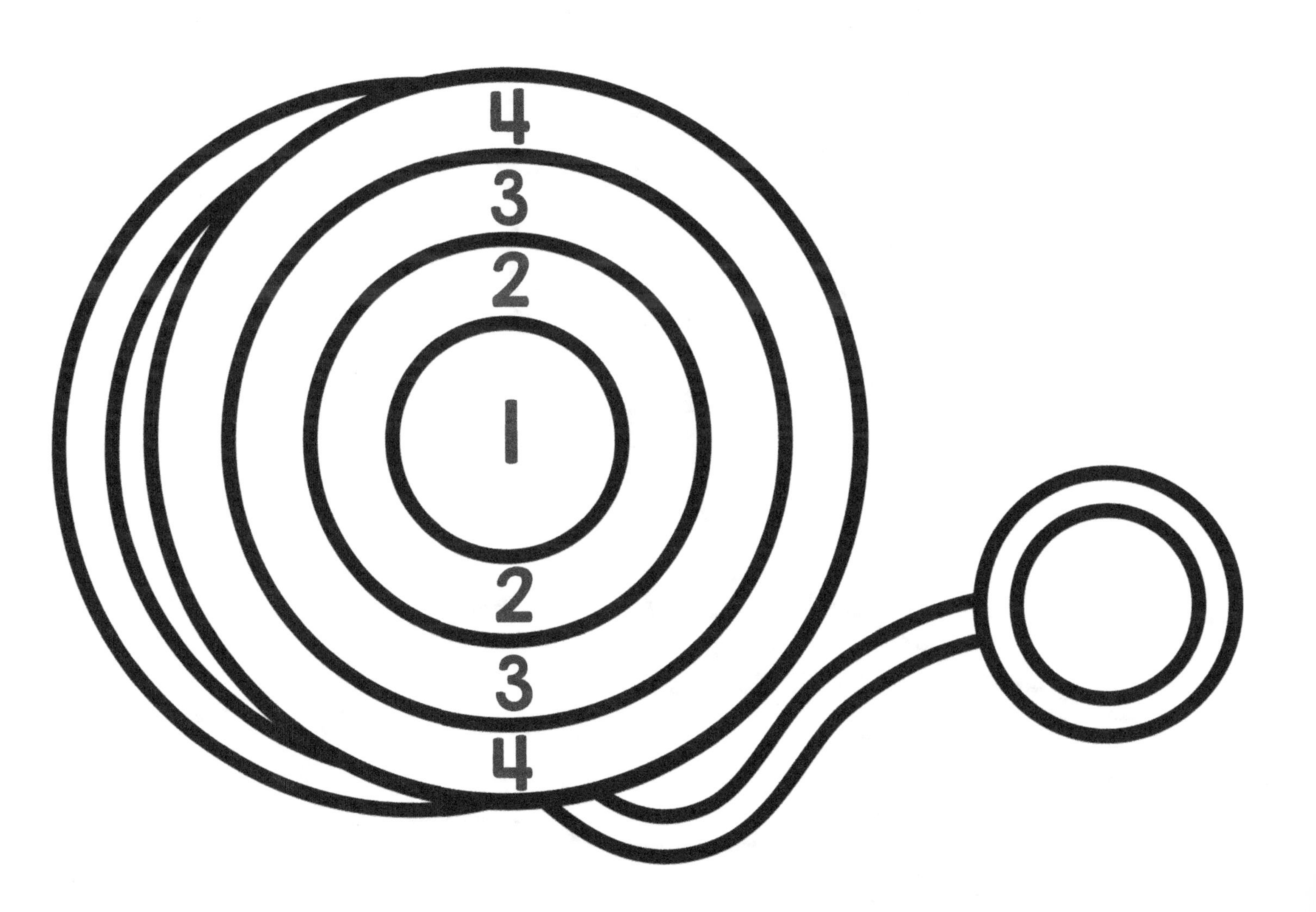
4
3
2
1
2
3
4

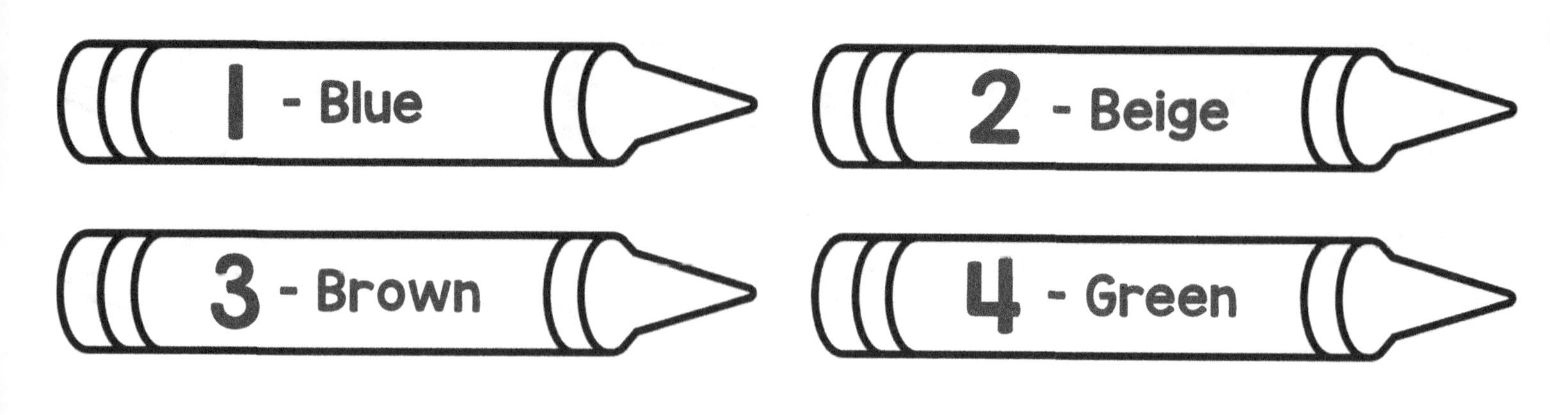
1 - Blue
2 - Beige
3 - Brown
4 - Green

4
4
4
4
4
4
3
2
1

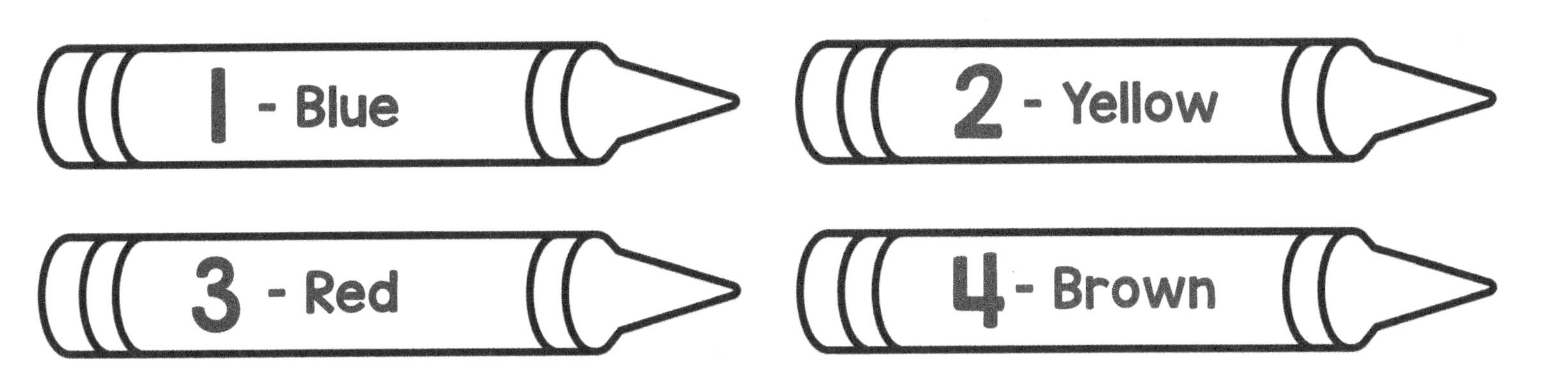
1 - Blue
2 - Yellow
3 - Red
4 - Brown

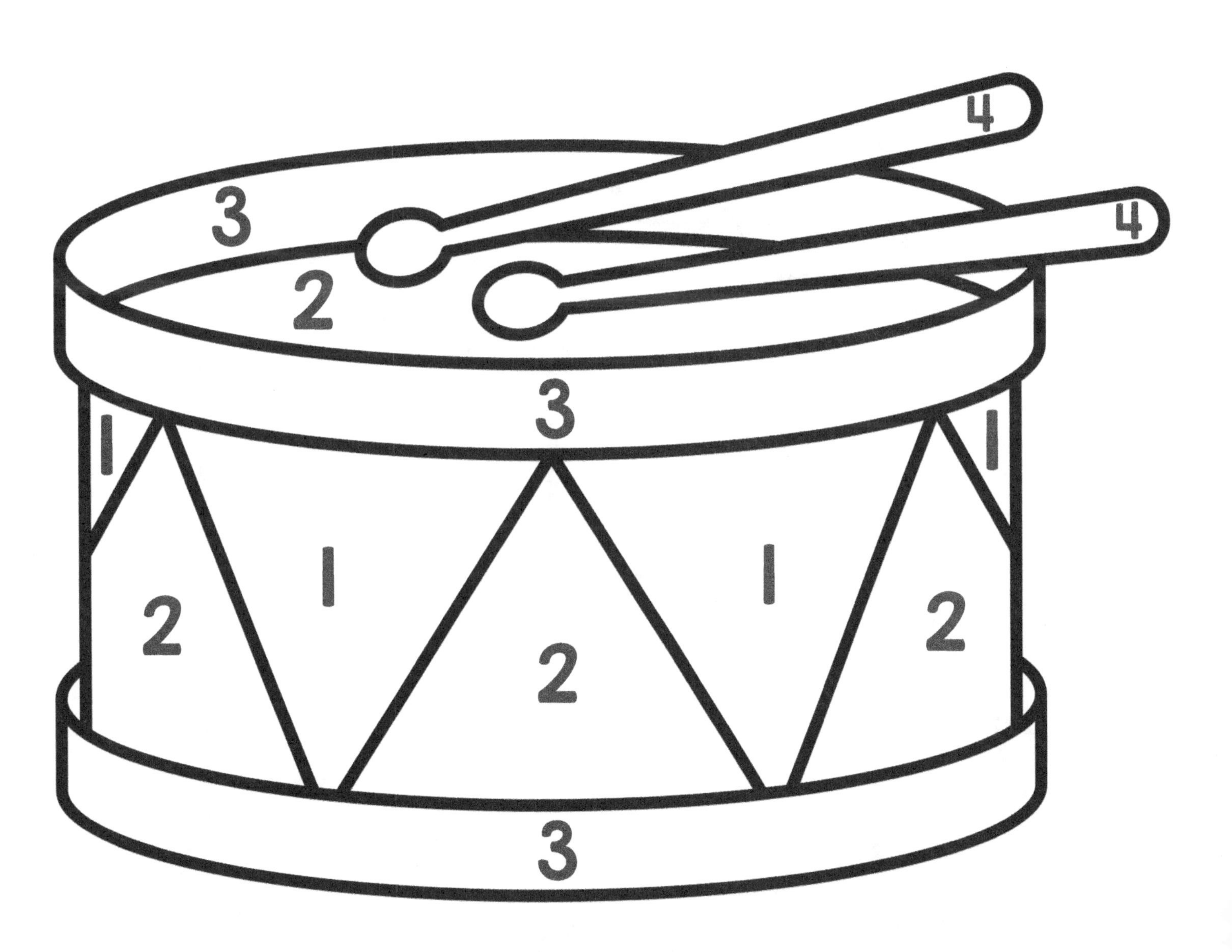
4
4
3
2
3
1
1
1
1
2
2
2
3

1 - Red
2 - Orange
3 - Black
4 - Gray
4
2
2
1
2
4
2
1
4
3
4
3
4
3
4

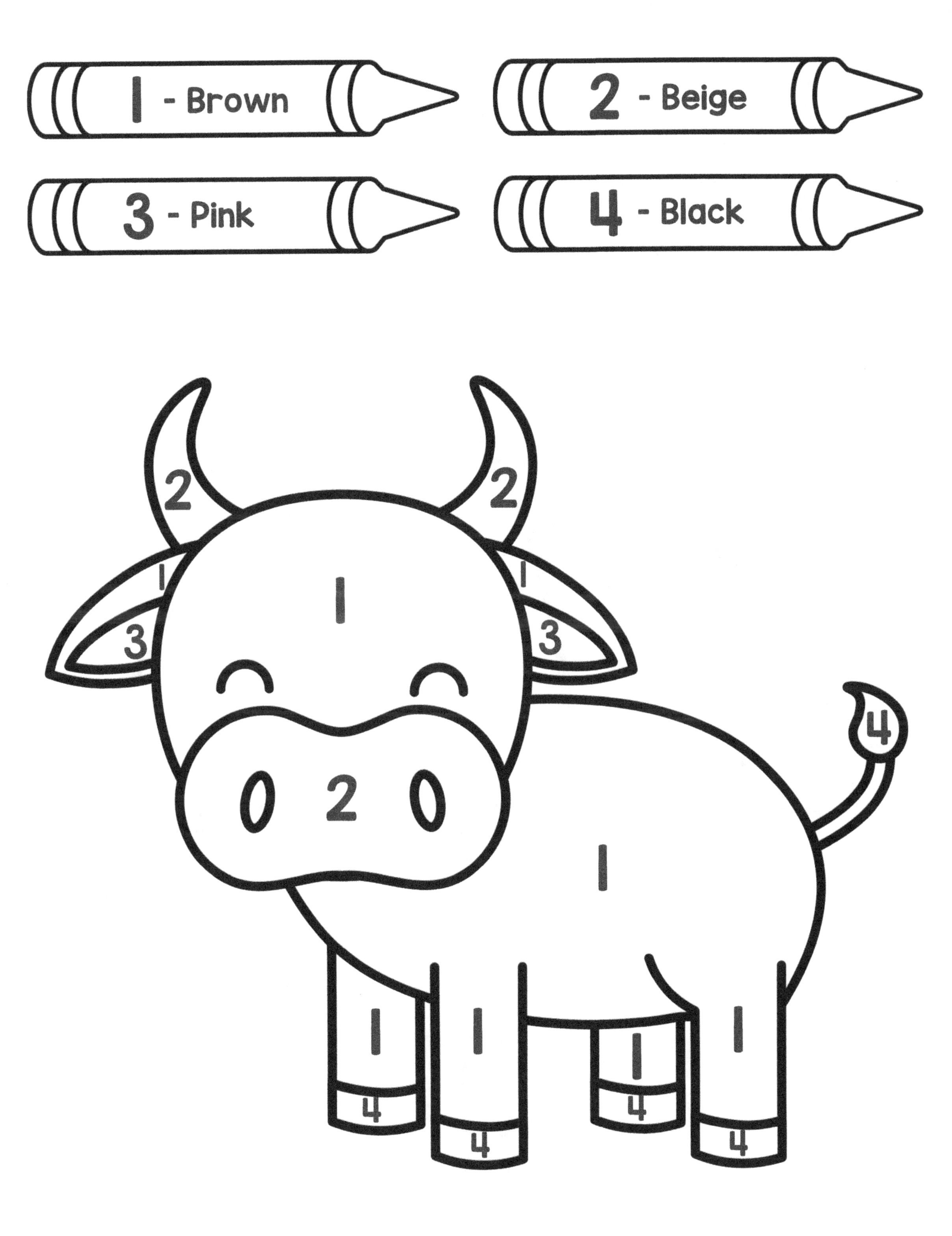
1 - Brown
2 - Beige
3 - Pink
4 - Black
2
2
1
1
1
3
3
4
2
1
1
1
1
1
4
4
4
4

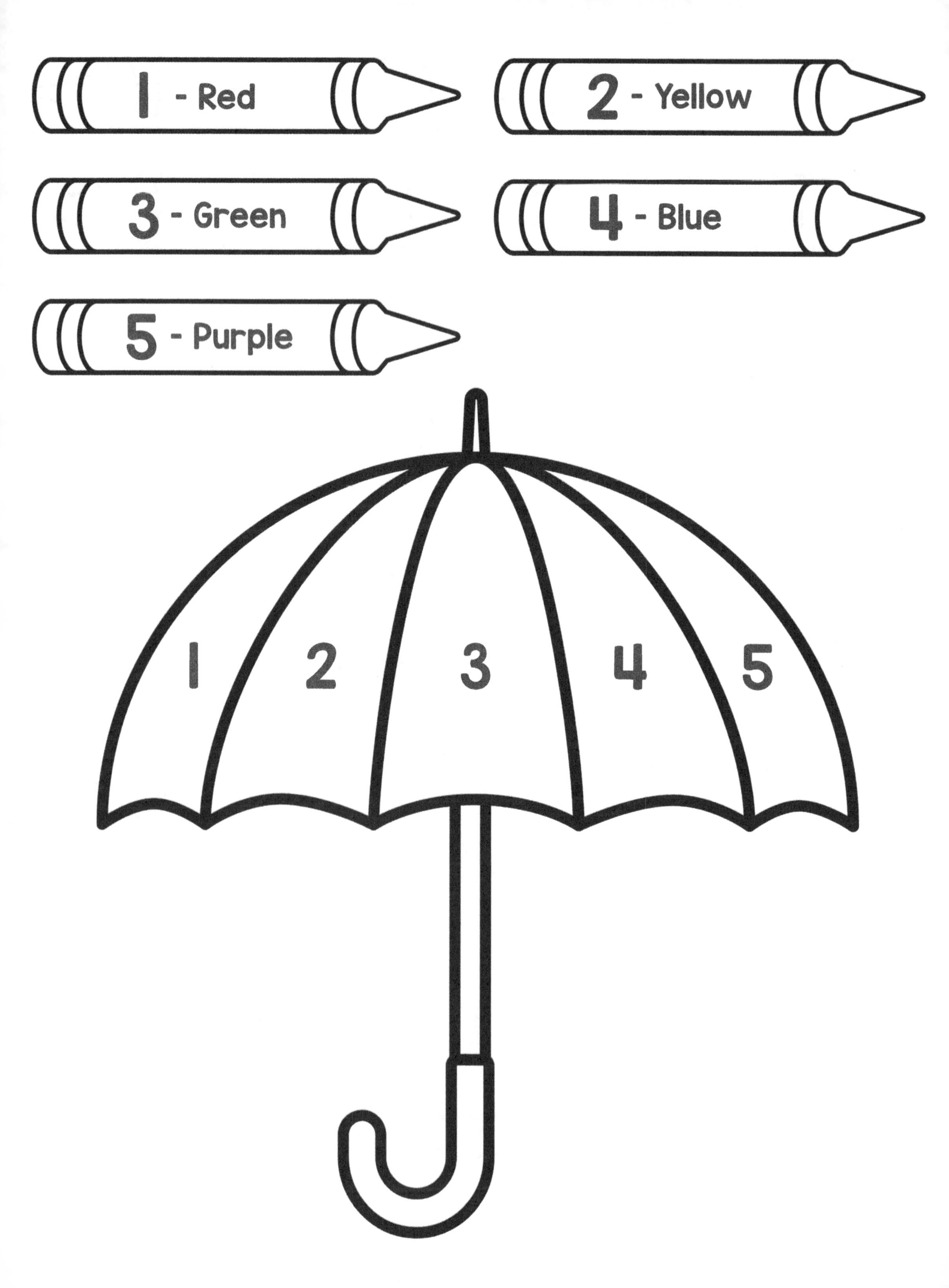
1 - Red
2 - Yellow
3 - Green
4 - Blue
5 - Purple
1
2
3
4
5

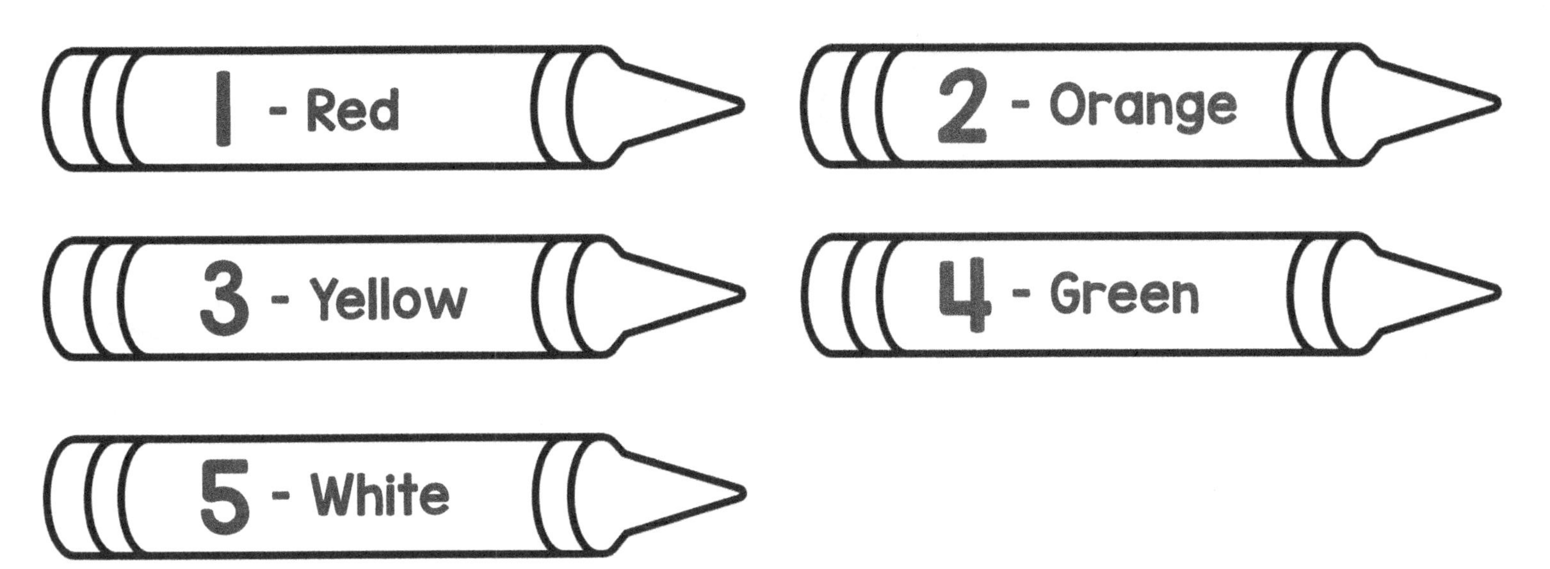
1 - Red
2 - Orange
3 - Yellow
4 - Green
5 - White

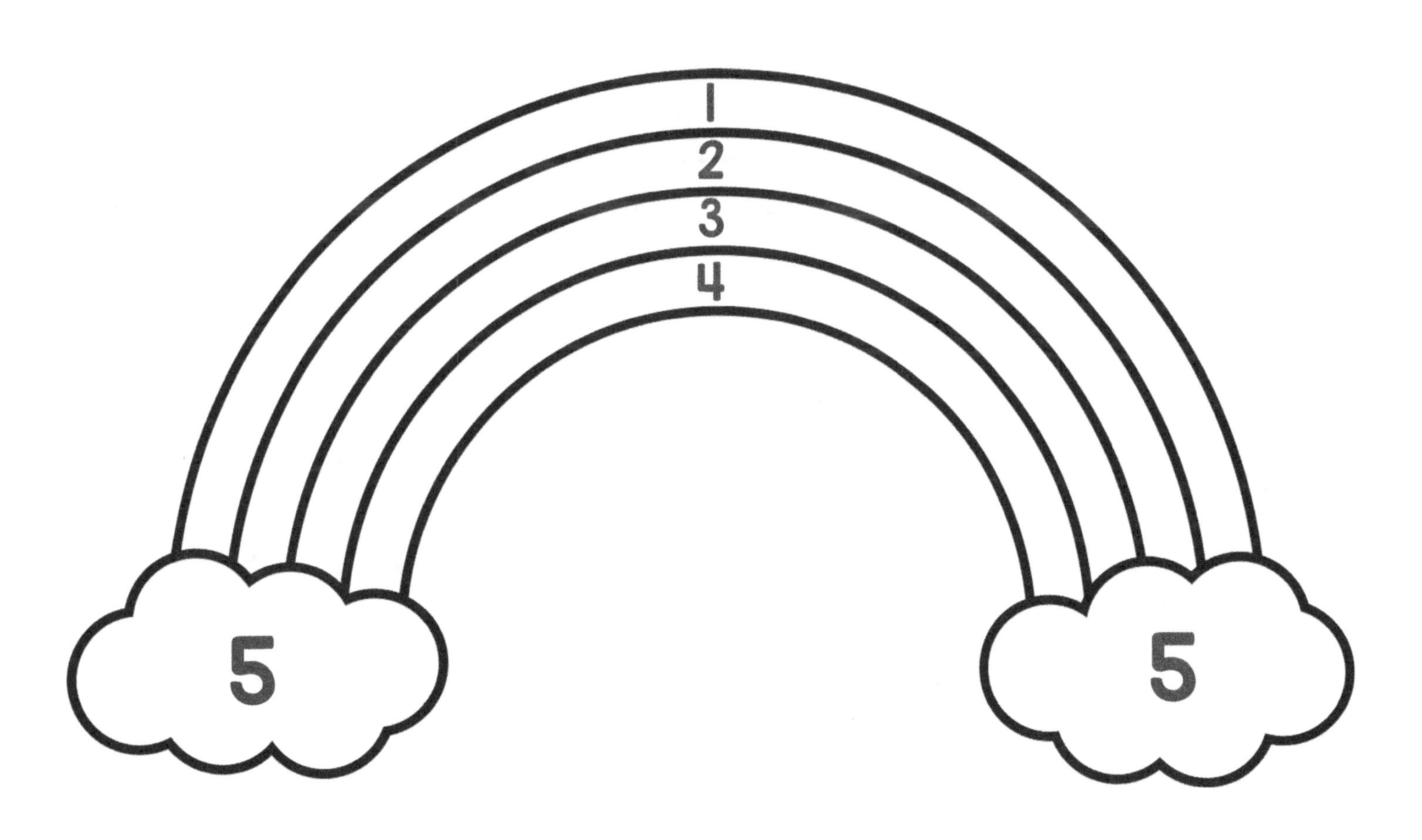
1
2
3
4
5
5

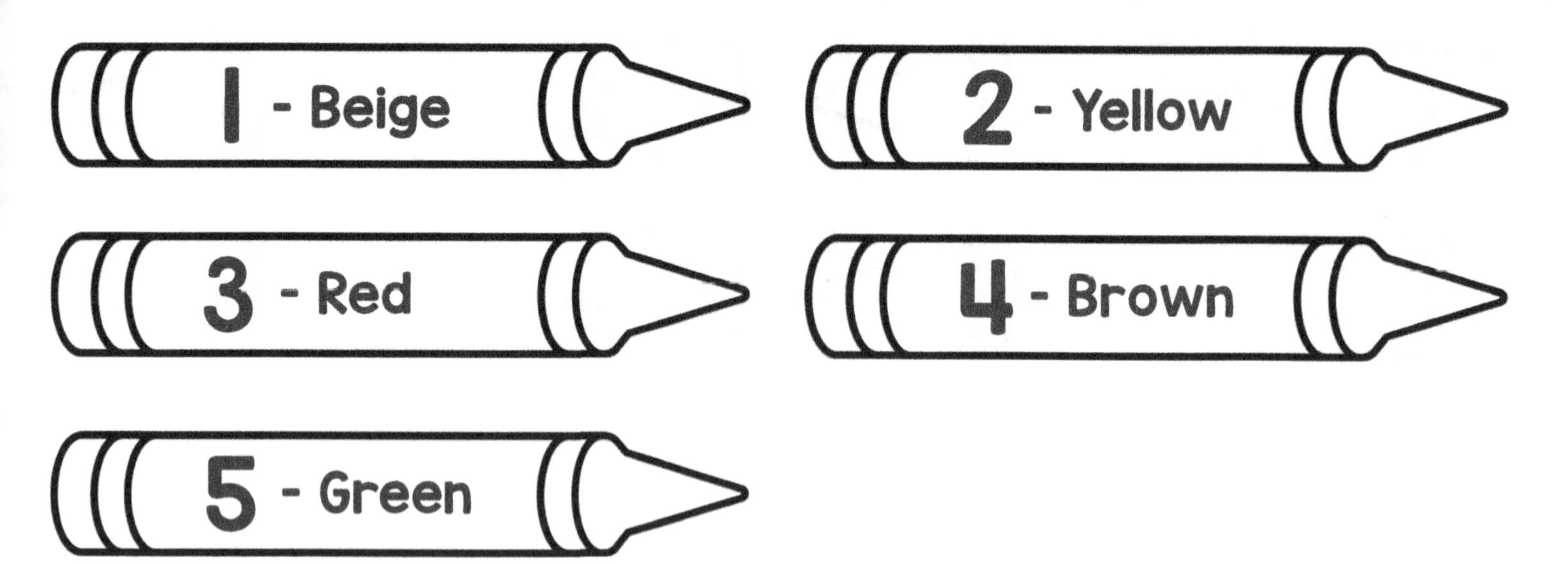
1 - Beige
2 - Yellow
3 - Red
4 - Brown
5 - Green

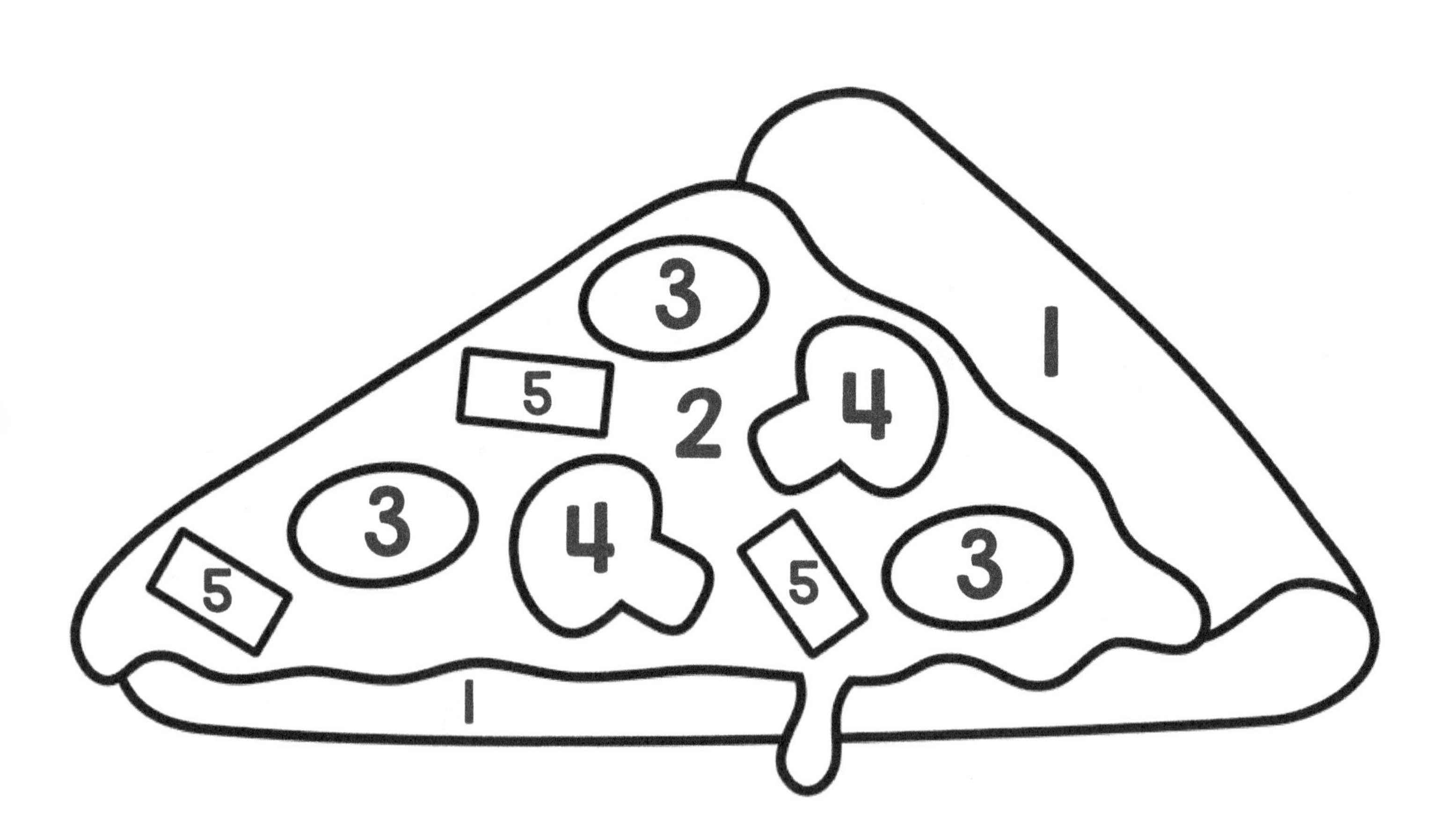
3
5
2
4
1
3
4
5
3
5
1

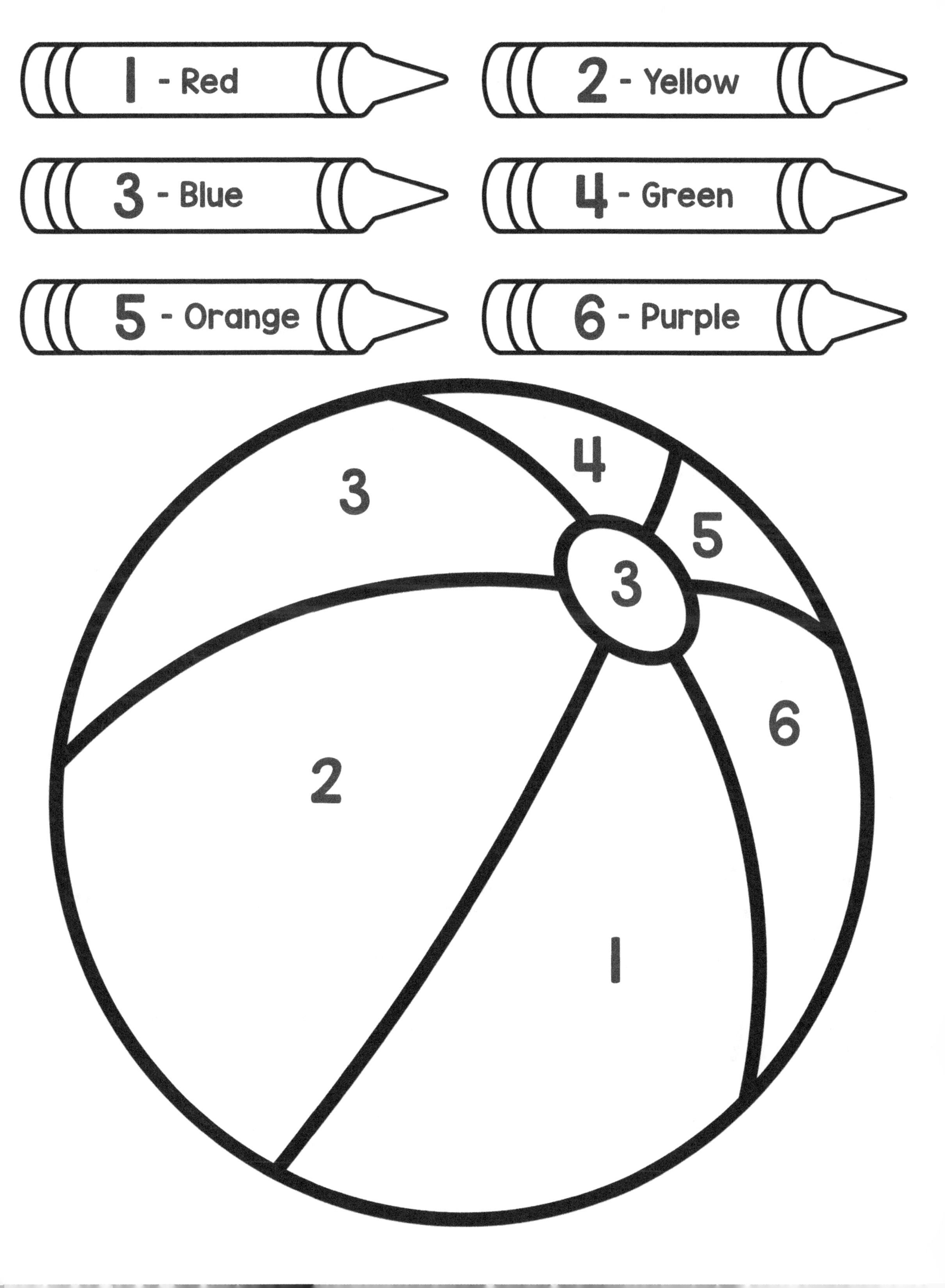
1 - Red
2 - Yellow
3 - Blue
4 - Green
5 - Orange
6 - Purple
3
4
5
3
6
2
1

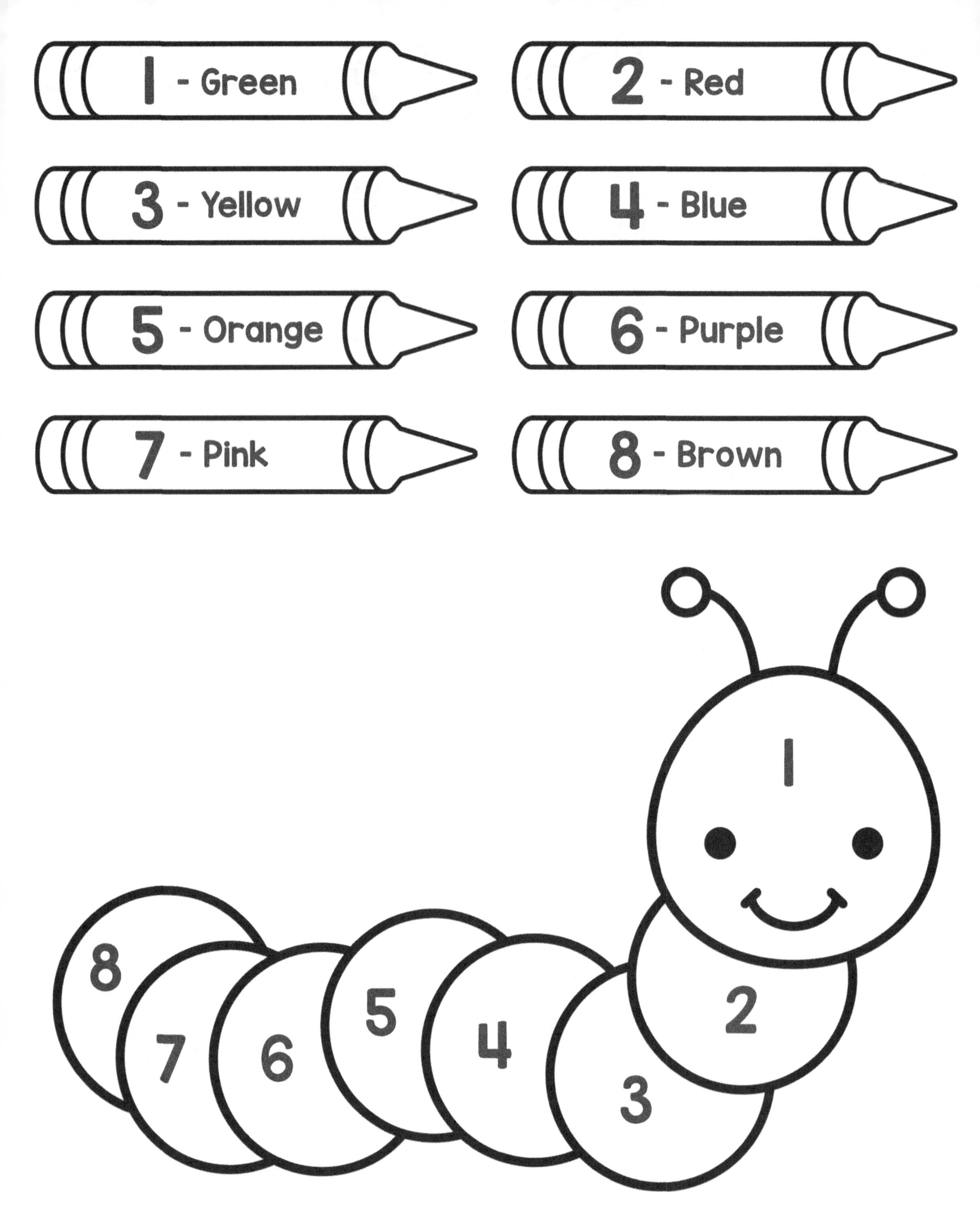
1 - Green
2 - Red
3 - Yellow
4 - Blue
5 - Orange
6 - Purple
7 - Pink
8 - Brown
1
2
3
4
5
6
7
8

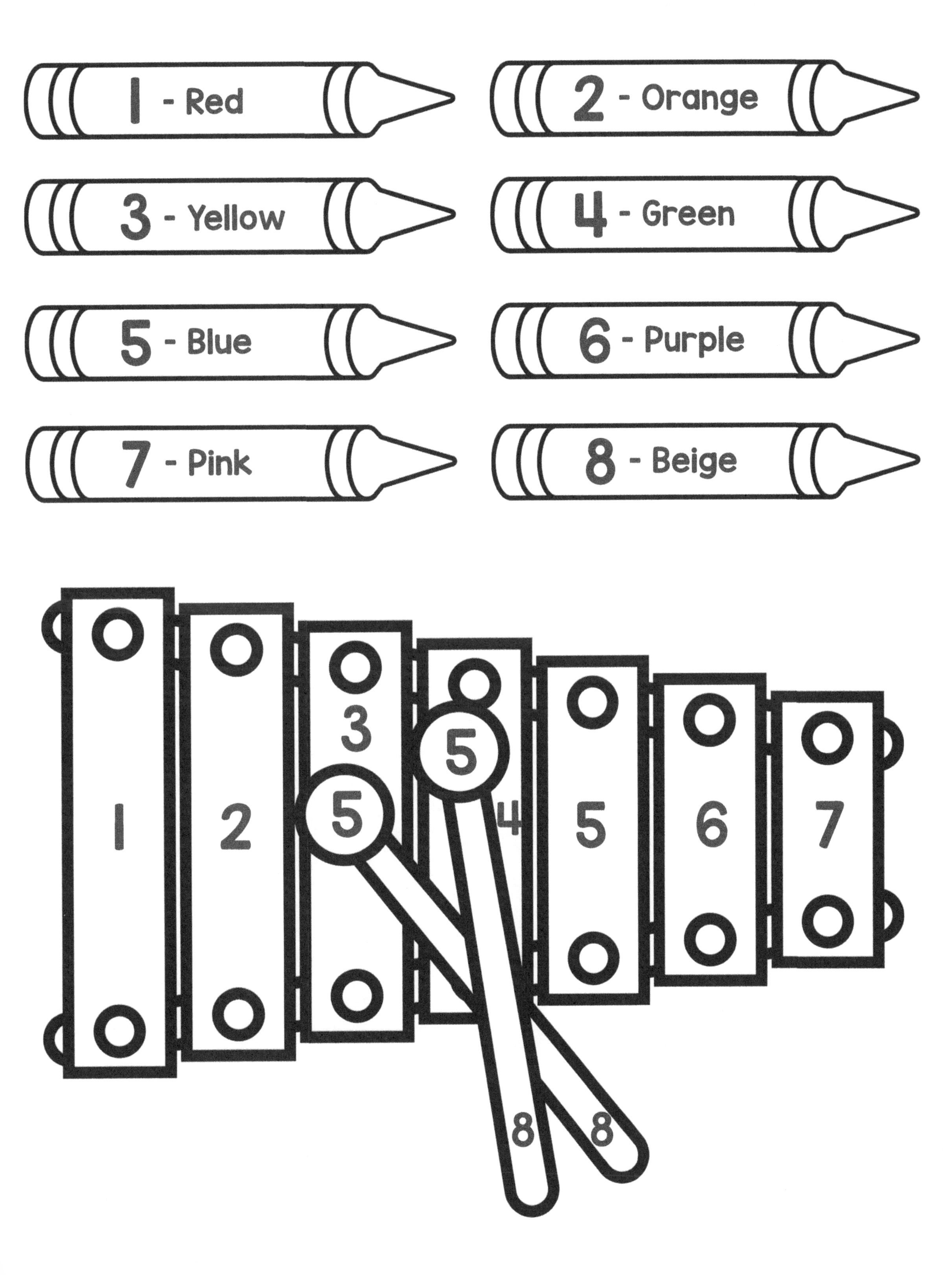
1 - Red
2 - Orange
3 - Yellow
4 - Green
5 - Blue
6 - Purple
7 - Pink
8 - Beige
1
2
3
4
5
5
5
6
7
8
8

Made in the USA
Middletown, DE
06 September 2024

60503632R00031